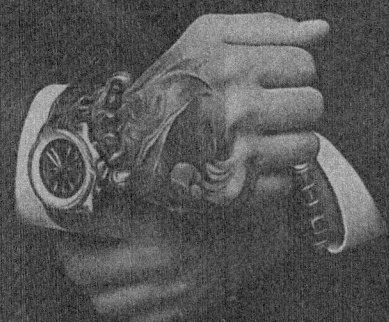

A REVERSE HAREM NOVEL

SCARS

BOOK ONE IN THE TRIAD SERIES

DANA ISALY

SCARS
Copyright © 2021 Dana Isaly
All rights reserved.
Published: Dana Isaly 2021

No parts of this book may be reproduced in any form without written consent from the author. Except in the use of brief quotations in a book review.
This book is a piece of fiction. Any names, characters, businesses, places or events are a product of the author's imagination or are used fictitiously. Any resemblance to persons living or dead, events or locations is purely coincidental.
This book is licensed for your personal enjoyment only. This book may not be resold or given away to other people. If you are reading this book and have not purchased it for your use only, then you should return it to your favorite book retailer and purchase your own copy.
Thank you for respecting the author's work.

Editing: Sandra at One Love Editing
Cover Design: Pink Elephant Designs
Formatting: Pink Elephant Designs

This book is dedicated to myself ten years ago, writing smut in secret, not realizing there was a whole genre for this shit. Look at yourself now, girl.

Also, if you're a family member of mine, put this book down immediately. This one is not for you. Please. I beg you. Put. It. Down.

AUTHOR'S *note*

A short note to make you aware of any triggers this book may have for you. There is a lot of swearing, quite a bit of violence, and a lot of sex. There is a scene that depicts sexual assault.

CHAPTER *one*

SCARLET

It was called Hell House for a reason. An entire family was supposedly murdered within its walls like our own version of *The Amityville Horror*. I honestly had no idea if that was true. I wasn't there for the ghosts; I was there for the party. People brought generators and enough alcohol and drugs to take care of an entire town.

Not that I would ever partake in the hard shit. I might look rough, but I was not about to catch a charge for a night of fun. Weed was as far as I'd take it.

I threw the joint on the ground and crushed it under my black Doc Martens. Blowing out the last of the smoke into the cold air, I smiled at the raging house party going on in front of me. People were spilling out onto the front yard, stumbling and yelling, some practically fucking through their clothes.

"I heard *they're* coming tonight," Kenna said next to me.

"You think they're coming all the way on this side of the city just for a shitty little house party?" I raised one dark brow at her and shook my head. "*Ei căcat.*" Sometimes I just preferred swearing in Romanian. It rolled off my tongue with more of a bite than English did.

She took a drink from her beer and shrugged. "Rumor is they've got some business to take care of."

A little thrill went through me at the thought of what violence that promised. If they had business to take care of, that probably meant they would be beating the ever-living shit out of some poor soul who had crossed them.

"Well, that would definitely make for a fun night."

Kenna laughed and downed the rest of her beer. "You're a sick fuck, Scarlet."

I shrugged. "Growing up the way I did, you get used to that kind of violence."

She side-eyed me but didn't ask the questions she was always dying to. Kenna and I had been friends for about a year, but she didn't know anything about my past other than it wasn't your regular run-of-the-mill childhood. And I intended to keep it that way. Keep her clueless, keep her safe.

"Look, this is my one night off this week," I said, slinging my arm around her shoulders. "Can we please go back inside, get absolutely shitfaced, and find some poor unsuspecting men or women to grind on?"

She smiled, and her brown eyes lit up. Her hand grasped mine on her shoulder, making my rings dig into my fingers painfully, but I squeezed back.

We made our way across the lawn, dodging the drunk and disorderly. Kenna's arm slinked around my waist, and our hips swayed in time with each other as we made our way inside. "Bodies" by Drowning Pool started up as we made our way to what used to be a massive dining room. A mosh pit was quickly forming in the middle of it, and I pulled Kenna along with me right into the center.

One of the perks of being short was that I could usually push my way through the crowds with my lower center of gravity and not be pushed to the floor. When we found our way to the dead center, we were in a tangle of fists, arms, and torsos. I screamed the lyrics, throwing my own body around like I was a doll, my black hair whipping my face.

This was the reason I was wearing jeans and not a dress. You didn't wear skimpy clothing when you were going to be in the middle of a mosh pit with thirty other people. Kenna's face was red and hot with exertion when I looked over at her, where she was grinding on some metalhead behind her. Her dark hair fell in wild tangles around her tattooed shoulders. His fingertips dug into her waist as they moved together. I licked my lips.

I grabbed her face and brought my mouth to her ear.

"You beautiful bitch!" I heard her laugh, and I caught it with my mouth, our lips meeting with bruising force. We broke apart, and I screamed the song with the rest of the crowd into the air.

After the song had ended, my voice was raw, and my body was well and truly bruised. I had never felt more alive. Kenna dismissed the guy with a wave of her hand, and I smiled as she pulled me close. Sometimes I was seriously in awe of how lucky I was to have stumbled across her.

"Let's go get a drink. If I stay in here much longer, I'm going home with broken bones. These assholes are crazy." I took her hand, and we made our way to the old kitchen. The music was still blasting, but it was a bit quieter on that side of the house. A few people were making out in the dark corners, but mostly everyone was just drinking and talking. Kenna sank to the floor and dug through the bottom shelves. Then half of her body suddenly disappeared under the counter.

"The fuck are you doing?"

"Last time we were here," she said, her voice muffled, "I broke through one of these to hide a bottle of—" She popped out, bottle in hand. "—whiskey!" She cracked it open and took a long swig before handing it over to me. The familiar burn comforted my already sore body. We both jumped up on the counter, drinking in silence and watching the couple in the corner.

"Think they'll just fuck right there against the wall?" Kenna licked the drop of alcohol off her bottom lip, and

I could feel my stomach tighten at the gesture. I peeled my eyes off her mouth and looked at the couple in the corner. The guy had the girl pressed up against the wall, her legs around his waist. Her dress was completely up around her hips. "I wouldn't fuck anyone in this house even if you paid me. This place is disgusting."

"Don't be such a snob. Sometimes it's nice to get a little dirty." I wagged my eyebrows at her, and she just rolled her eyes.

"Scarlet, you fuck anything that moves. I wouldn't be surprised to find you up against one of these walls one day." Any other person may have taken offense at Kenna's words, but she wasn't wrong. Ever since I was a kid, I knew I thought both boys and girls were cute. And growing up in the type of family I did, you learned to get your rocks off while you still could, with who you could. I never knew what day would be my last. I instinctively reached up and tapped my fingers against the jagged scar along my jaw.

Before I could come back with a snarky remark, a commotion broke out in the front of the house. Kenna's hand flew to my thigh, and I tried to fight against what that did to my body. This woman was going to be the death of me. Kenna was so straight she might as well have been a ruler. No matter how badly I wanted to convince her into experimenting, I wouldn't ever push her to do something she wasn't comfortable with. I was content just being her friend with a few stolen kisses here and there.

But that didn't mean my body listened.

"I'm sure it's nothing, Kenna," I said, taking her hand off my thigh. "Just chill here. I'll go check it out."

"You are so not leaving me alone in this dingy-ass kitchen, Scarlet."

I rolled my eyes as she hopped off the counter and followed me out. The whole place was horribly lit, seeing as the generators could only do so much for a house this big. We snuck through the hallways, pushing up against the walls and out of the way of everyone going the exact opposite way we were. The exact opposite way of where the commotion was.

That was exciting.

"Do you think they're here? Who do you think they're coming for?" Kenna's voice was a whisper, and I could barely make it out under all the noise.

"Some sorry ass that wronged them, their business, or someone that has paid them…handsomely." Kenna's hand found mine again and squeezed against the metal covering mine. "It'll be fine, Kenna. They aren't coming for us." I turned back to her, stopping next to the stairs. "Unless you have some sort of underground drug cartel you're part of that I don't know about?"

She gave me a quick shove, and I laughed but kept us moving through the house. Everyone was either pushing past us to get out of the way or crowding around what used to be the dance floor just a few moments ago. I walked up to the first guy in the crowd that I saw and tapped him on the back.

"Help a girl out?" I asked, gesturing for him to give me a boost. He gave me a stupid crooked grin.

"Anything for you, baby."

I smiled, holding back my gag reflex. I hated being called baby. I was not a child. He held his hands out in a little cup shape, and I thanked whatever gods there were that I used to be a cheerleader and knew how to hoist myself up. My heavy boot landed in his hands, and I swung my other leg up and over his shoulder.

Next to me, Kenna got in a similar position on another guy. The room had completely cleared out except for *them*. The Triad. There they were in all their muscled, tattooed glory, stalking around, waiting for someone to turn the music off. Their leader—I didn't know any of their names—sat against a windowsill, twisting the rings on his fingers. His hair was bleach blond, almost white. One bulky East Asian with his long, silky hair pulled into a knot on his head stood next to Blondie with his arms crossed. The brunet with the nose ring paced in a circle like he had better places to be, his heavy boots clumping across the wooden floor.

"Fuck me, they're beautiful," Kenna whispered over to me. I rolled my eyes. She wasn't wrong. But I had grown up with this brand of asshole.

"Don't drool on that poor man's head, Ken." I winked at her, and the guy below her looked up like he was actually worried she was drooling over these idiots.

The music cut off, and the entire house went quiet. The guy that was pacing came to a stop, and all attention landed on Blondie as he stood up and made his way to the center of the circle we had all formed.

"We're looking for someone we think is here tonight. If anyone knows them, we expect you to give us information. We'll pay you handsomely." God, his voice was rough as gravel. I was sucked in against my will. I couldn't take my eyes off of the way his muscles moved under the idiotically tight black tee he was wearing. "If you're here, princess," he said, pausing to look around the room, "we would appreciate you coming forward without any trouble."

Kenna and I looked at each other.

"They're here for a girl?" she mouthed at me. My stomach dropped. It couldn't be.

"But we do like a good chase," Man Bun mumbled under his breath. My own breath was coming in and out too quickly. I could feel the color draining from my face.

Fuck. Fuck. Fuck.

"Miss Scarlet," he started to say. But before my name was out of his mouth, I had pulled myself free from dude's shoulders and fallen straight onto the floor. The wind was knocked out of my lungs, but I knew I had to go. Kenna jumped onto the ground.

"Are you okay?" she asked just a little too loudly.

"There she is," I heard one of the guys singsong. I grabbed Kenna's hand.

"Fucking run, Kenna," I said and pulled her along behind me. I felt the sea of people behind us part, but I was already out the door. I pulled the knife out of my back pocket and flicked it open. Running with sharp objects wasn't smart. But when you had three reapers trailing you, and quickly, it was a risk one had to take.

We made it out onto the front lawn, and I pulled

her to the right and aimed for the woods. If we could just get far enough in, we could lose them.

"What the fucking fuck, Scarlet! Do you have a bounty on your head or something?" Kenna whispered through gritted teeth. Our breaths were coming fast and short. The boots I had chosen were not great for running. I was essentially running with cinder blocks on.

"Long story. Tell you once we get out of this alive, yeah?" She nodded in agreement.

I could feel them gaining on us. Not surprising seeing as I was all of five feet on a good day and they were all well over six feet and trained killing machines.

"No sense in running, precious!" one of them said way too close to my ear. He wasn't even out of breath. Adrenaline kicked in, and I pushed with all my might. I swung my arm out, trying to slice him with the knife to slow him down. "That wasn't very nice!" I laughed, but he wasn't deterred. He reached out and grabbed my arm, twisting it painfully until I dropped the knife and went down with it. "Got ya!"

He grabbed the back of my flimsy tank, and I felt it rip on the way down. Fuck, that was one of my favorite tops.

Piercing guy was readily on top of me, my arms behind my back. I looked up and saw Man Bun on top of Kenna and heard her whimpering. I fought against the hold on me.

"Let her go. She has nothing to do with this."

I heard leaves crunching, and then suddenly Blondie was crouching down in front of me. He grabbed my jaw, much harder than was necessary. That was definitely going to bruise.

"Yeah, you look like her alright. Scar and everything."

"Because I am her, asshole. Let my friend go. She has nothing to do with my family."

He shrugged and looked behind himself at Man Bun. He nodded towards him, and he got off Kenna. Relief flooded my system.

"Kenna, go," I grunted. "*O să fiu bine.*" I had taught her some Romanian. It made it easier to talk when we were in public seeing as no one ever understood it.

"But—" she started to protest, but Blondie cut her off.

"*Pleacă sau vei fi ucisă,* Kenna." I could almost feel him smile as he said it. My stomach dropped. They were most definitely sent by my family if he could speak and understand Romanian.

She looked at me briefly, tears filling up her eyes. But I nodded my head once, and she took off back towards the house.

"Alright, fuckers," I said now that it was just the four of us. "What's next?"

CHAPTER
two

SCARLET

"Alright, love. Are you going to come kindly, or are we going to fight all the way back to the car?"

I looked up into Blondie's face and smiled before spitting right in between his very green eyes. I laughed and then was hauled up onto my feet in one swift pull. My shoulders screamed, and I was very proud that I didn't.

"That's quite a mouth you've got on you, little one."

I pulled at my arms again, trying to get the blood moving in them, but it just made the one behind me pull me tighter against him. The sheer amount of muscle this guy had was infuriating.

"How much are they paying you?" Blondie wiped

my spit off his face with the bottom of his shirt, and Jesus wept. His entire stomach was covered in dark, intricate tattoos that moved across his hips and dipped down over that delicious vee and into his jeans. When I looked back up at his face, he held my stare with a smirk. Not ashamed of finding an attractive man attractive, I held his gaze with my own smile. It's not like I'd have to deal with them much longer. I was not going to be handed over like a prized cow. I just had to figure out how to get away first.

"Nothing yet, princess." That caught me off guard, and my face instantly betrayed my confusion. "Not what you were expecting? We're full of surprises." Dude behind me zip-tied my wrists, gently I noticed, as I stood there in a stare-off with Blondie. "Seb," he said with a grin. "You want the honors, seeing as she drew blood?"

I looked down at his arm and saw I had cut him pretty good. Blood was dripping down the outside of his forearm and down his fingers. I snorted and looked back at him.

"Oops."

His dark eyes lit up with amusement as he laughed at me. Okay, maybe these guys *were* full of surprises. That was not the reaction I was expecting either. His bloody hand reached up and marked my cheek. I fought against the warring feelings that caused. I couldn't decide if I was revolted that some stranger's blood was suddenly smeared across my cheek or if I was turned on.

Yeah, I was fucked-up. And he saw it. Those dark eyes held mine for just a moment too long.

"Let's go, little one." He bent over and threw me over his shoulder like a sack of potatoes, making my face bounce off his hip. Then he swatted my ass. Hard.

"Motherfucker," I swore against the sharp pain in my nose.

"Motherfucker sounds so sweet coming out of your mouth, but my name is Sebastian, sweetheart." I grunted as we started walking back towards the house.

"And Man Bun and Blondie back there?" I couldn't see them from my current position, but I could hear them mumbling to each other.

"Elliot and Tristan. Respectively."

"What a delight it is to meet you all." Sebastian laughed again, and it vibrated through me. "Where are we going? If my family isn't paying you to get me, then why are you here?"

"You ask a lot of questions for someone in your position," one of the boys behind us said. Someone was grumpy.

"You'll have to excuse Elliot, darling. He's always been a little moody." Elliot scoffed, and Tristan walked up closer to me so that I could turn my head and look up at him. The blood was rushing to my head, and that mixed with the alcohol was already giving me a headache. "You see, Scarlet, when we got word that you were hiding out in our city, we thought it might be smart to capitalize on the opportunity."

The motion of my head bobbing and my body

moving with Sebastian's steps was going to make me sick. I looked back down at the ground and closed my eyes.

"So, you haven't spoken to my family? They don't know where I am?"

"Not yet. But we've heard they've been looking for you. You've been in hiding for quite a while, haven't you? Disappeared on your twenty-first birthday and you're, what? Twenty-three now?"

"Twenty-four."

"You had a good run. But I would prefer you not be found in our city. It could look like we're harboring a fugitive and cause an all-out gang war between us and your family. So we are going to happily turn you over. And I'm betting they'll be willing to pay good money for you."

"Oh, I'm sure they will. Either that or they'll just have you off me yourself." Sebastian stopped and dropped me to my feet. I swayed a moment before catching my balance. We weren't back in front of the house. We were on the old dirt road that led to it. They had pulled over and hidden the idling car among the trees.

Sebastian opened the back door and easily picked me up and put me on the seat. There was an older man sitting in the driver's seat, staring straight ahead like he wasn't allowed to look at me.

"Scoot to the middle for me, love."

"Ugh," I groaned as I shifted over. "Enough with the little pet names."

Sebastian laughed and took off his shirt to wrap his

forearm as he slid into the car. Fuck me, this was going to be a long ride if I had to sit next to those abs the entire time.

Elliot, the grump, opened the other door and sat on my other side. Where Sebastian let our bodies touch and sat a little too close for comfort, Elliot made sure his body was pressed firmly against the door instead. Once Tristan was in the front seat, we were off.

I shifted my attention over to Sebastian since he seemed to be the nicest of the group—and not hard to look at in his current state of undress. He looked down at me and grinned, throwing his arm around the seat behind me. His fingers found strands of my hair, and he twisted them over and over.

"Yes, love?"

I rolled my eyes. "Can you tell me where we are going?"

"He cannot," Elliot grunted.

"I didn't ask you, big boy. I asked Sebastian. Don't speak unless spoken to. First rule of good manners." Suddenly my entire throat was wrapped in his hand, tightly. He gripped it and dug his fingers into my neck, and the immediate pain and lack of oxygen made my eyes water.

"Listen here, little girl. I eat bitches like you for breakfast. Shut the fuck up and sit there like the pretty little princess you are." He let go and pushed me back. I fell into Sebastian, and his arm landed around my shoulders and stayed there.

"If you wanted to get me in bed, Man Bun, all you had to do was ask. I like it a bit rough" I rolled my neck as Elliot swore under his breath and turned his stare out the window, sinking further into the door than I thought was possible. Sebastian's hand came around my throat, and I froze, thinking he was going to bruise it even further.

"Are you alright, little one?" he murmured into my ear so only I could hear. Yea, Sebastian was definitely the cinnamon roll of the group. He gently traced his fingertips over my skin, and I cursed myself for the gooseflesh that it caused. My piece-of-shit body was constantly acting up when I didn't need it to be. I squeezed my thighs together and prayed he didn't notice.

I nodded once, afraid of what my voice might sound like if I spoke. His fingers dipped lower onto my collarbone and traced the dark outlines of my chest tattoo. And then lower.

"Seb, quit playing with the new toy, please." Tristan's voice was like a bucket of cold water. I had literally just been kidnapped. And here I was like a bitch in heat from a few soft touches on my bruised neck.

"But she's so feisty, and her body responds so nicely," Sebastian said into my hair. "Look at that blush."

"Regardless, hands off." Tristan's face was like stone. "She's off-limits."

"If you're worried about damaged goods, I can assure you that ship sailed quite a long time ago."

Tristan just looked at me and then turned back around.

"We're taking you to one of our safe houses," Sebastian said as he took his arm off my shoulders.

"What the fuck, Seb!" Elliot whipped his face around. His expression was almost cartoonish in his anger. I expected his head to explode any second.

"Oh, please, Elliot. Me telling her we are taking her to a safe house tells her literally nothing. We're blindfolding her once we get on the main road."

"Stop bickering like a married couple or I will separate you," Tristan sang from the front seat.

"Well, alright then. Can we at least stop and get some food on the way there? I'm dealing with a belly full of liquor and not much else, fellas. A girl's got to eat."

Tristan sighed and laid his head back against the headrest. He and the other two boys discussed food options like I wasn't there. By the time we had made it to the main highway, Tristan produced a blindfold that Sebastian wrapped around my eyes.

"Can you see anything, pet?"

I groaned. This boy and his little names. "Nope. All dark, no stars, sunshine."

His low laughter vibrated through me in a way I was not mentally okay with.

"Alright, let's get you home and get you some food, then." He kissed my cheek.

I figured I had pushed them all enough for the duration of the car ride and sat in silence. And listened. I listened to them talk about food, about the party, the vague details of their day tomorrow, and what they were going to do with me. Because growing up in a family like mine, you learned to always be listening.

The smallest details could come to be the most important ones later on.

And if I was going to escape these three so that I could get away from my family again, every little detail mattered.

CHAPTER
three

SCARLET

I fell asleep at some point because I woke up to being forcefully pushed off a shoulder as I fell into another one. And when I opened my eyes, I could see. Thankfully, the blindfold had been removed. I sat up and looked around. We were pulling into a long gravel driveway that was surrounded on both sides by heavy forest.

"You snore," Elliot said.

I whipped my head around to him. "I do not. And you didn't have to shove me off of you so violently."

He gave me a smirk.

"Yes, you do," Tristan chimed in from the front seat, still texting away on his phone.

"It's okay, precious. Something so loud coming out of something so little was absolutely adorable." I moved like I was going to flip Sebastian off, but the sharp sting of muscles that had been bound for too long reminded me of my current state.

"I don't have any weapons. Can we please cut these fucking things off of my wrists before I lose my hands?"

We pulled up to a wrought iron gate, and the old man rolled down the window and spoke to someone on the other side of the speaker.

"Go ahead, Seb." Tristan caught my eye in the rearview mirror and winked. "She's been a good girl." I stuck my tongue out at him, the worst gesture I could do with my hands still tied behind my back. "Be careful, Scarlet. Stick your tongue out again and I might be inclined to find something it can lick. Especially with that tongue piercing. What a nice little surprise that is."

I clamped my mouth shut so tightly I tasted blood. The gates opened, and we started moving further down the road.

"Fuck you. I would bite your dick off if you put it anywhere near my mouth."

Sebastian cut my hands free, and I slowly massaged my arms to get the blood moving. Fuck, that was painful. Tristan ran a hand through his blond hair and laughed.

"Don't make promises you can't keep."

I rolled my eyes at him and bit back another snarky remark. I needed them to trust me, not hate me.

I watched as the safe house came into view. It was still pitch-black outside, so I didn't think we had been traveling for very long. A mansion that could have belonged in something like *Pride and Prejudice* rolled into view. Don't get me wrong, my family was wealthy, very wealthy, so I was always in mansions and penthouses. The rich and their desire to show everyone their wealth was a universal trend.

But I didn't think a safe house would be so lavish. And I definitely didn't think I would be afforded any type of comfort like this.

"Christ," I breathed, not really talking to any of them.

"Just wait until you see your room, little one," Sebastian murmured into my ear. This guy had no idea what personal space was.

"Although I am reconsidering how close we put you to all of us after hearing you snore like a chainsaw for the past hour." With my hands free, I was able to smile and flip Tristan off with both hands, but he just grinned.

"I don't snore," I mumbled.

We pulled to a stop in front of the house, and everyone climbed out, but I just sat there and looked up at the building. Sebastian smiled when he realized I wasn't moving and leaned back in through the door. He licked his lips and looked me up and down. My entire body heated under his gaze. It had been way too long since I'd gotten laid if my kidnapper was turning me on this much.

"You want me to throw you over my shoulder again, love?" God, he was too beautiful for his own good. And that Yorkshire accent was just about to do me in. My eyes traced down over his cheekbones and across the stubble forming on his jaw. I gave myself a mental kick and met his eyes again. His were filled with pure mischief.

"No, thank you. I can walk perfectly fine." I jumped out of the SUV and landed painfully on my feet. I was going to have so many blisters from running in brand-new boots.

"Seb, Elliot, go check the perimeter, and when you come inside, I want every exit personally checked by you both. It's been too long since the meatheads we have running this place have had such an important visitor."

Sebastian groaned. "But I wanted to be the one to show our pet her room!" he whined. He let out a curse when Elliot grabbed him by the back of the neck like a dog grabbing her pup. Sebastian's face shifted, and holy shit, I had never felt so much aggression roll off someone. Suddenly, the cinnamon roll was gone, and in its place was a predator. "Get your hands off of me, Elliot, or I will cause a scene in front of the lady."

Elliot rolled his eyes and gave him a push towards the side of the house.

A low growl made its way out of Sebastian's chest as he stalked over to me and grabbed my face in his hands. He squeezed me just a little too tight, and my body froze. I could feel him barely containing his anger. He licked my bottom lip, and my insides turned to jelly. I tried to pull back from him, but he held me too tightly.

"I'll come give you a tour tomorrow, pet," he said onto my mouth before letting go and stalking off in the other direction. My eyes closed, and I took a deep breath to get ahold of myself as he walked away. My body really needed to stop responding to violence this way.

"Report to me when you're done!" Tristan yelled after them, and Elliot raised his arm in confirmation.

I started shivering and bouncing on my toes. It was too fucking cold to just be standing around outside making small talk. Tristan looked at me, then down at my chest that was probably pushed up nicely by my crossed arms, and then back to my face. I couldn't see his facial expression well in the dim light, but I could feel the mood shift in him.

"Can we go inside, please?" I asked, trying to change the subject and get us moving. "I'm still in a ripped flimsy piece of fabric here." He gave a short laugh and motioned for me to follow him. He shoved his phone in the back pocket of his jeans and unlocked the front doors.

"No butlers?" I asked, making sure he could hear the sarcasm dripping off my mouth.

"It's three in the morning, Scarlet. What kind of employer would I be if I made my butler stay up this late just to let us inside?"

"A heartless gangster that kidnaps innocent women?"

All I got was an eye roll in response. He was harder to rile up than Elliot. I would just have to try harder in the future. When we walked inside, I was greeted by sweet, sweet warmth. Even for such a big house, it was nice and toasty inside. The front doors opened into a large foyer with double staircases. To the left looked like some sort of sitting room. The remnants of a fire still glowed. The other doors I could see were all shut. He threw his keys down on the stand next to the wall to our right and then stepped out of his boots.

"Shoes off," he said, pointing at my boots.

Holding my shirt to the front of me as I bent over, I unlaced them and slipped them off. I picked them up to take them upstairs with me, but he shook his head.

"These cost more money than I had to spend, asshole. I'm not leaving them lying around in a strange house."

"Scarlet, seriously. We are holding you for ransom and you think we are going to fuck with your shoes?" I shrugged and hugged them tighter to my chest. He sighed. "Fine. But don't let any dirt fall off of them and onto the carpet. It's new."

I followed him up the stairs, and he veered off to the right. We walked down too many hallways before getting to the room that was supposed to be mine. I was going to have to get out of there and explore if I was ever going to learn my way around and get the hell out of this place.

"We are all on this floor, on this hallway actually, and one of us will always be here." I knew a threat when I heard one, even if it was said with some politeness.

He opened the heavy wooden door and walked in first, flipping the lights on and checking in the closets, under the bed, and behind the curtains. He moved into the attached bathroom as I walked into the bedroom. All of the windows were covered in thick, velvet curtains, and the room had been painted black. The rest of the room was minimal, with exposed wood and some plants dotted around the room.

It was surprisingly cozy. I had expected a dark and drafty room with not much comfort, but that massive bed was calling my name like a siren song.

Tristan walked out of the bathroom.

"You reek of weed and alcohol. Take a shower before getting into bed. The guys decided while you were asleep that we would just make pizza here. I'll bring you some so that you can eat before you go to sleep. All of your clothes are here, and everything you need should already be stocked in the bathroom. If there's anything you find to be lacking, let one of us know and the housekeeper will make sure it's there tomorrow."

"Excuse me?" I said. "All of my clothes are here?"

He smiled, and those green eyes lit up. "Indeed they are, poppet. Went and got them myself before we came to get you at the party. I think this room should serve as an upgrade to the hovel you were living in." And with that, he left me alone. I didn't hear him lock the door, so I must have been allowed to move around the house as much as I wanted. For now.

I walked over and opened the closet. Sure enough, all my clothes were there. All of my shoes were organized on the floor, and all of my clothes were hung up. I opened the chest of drawers, and all of my bras and underwear were in there. Lovely. They had gone through my entire room. I made a mental note to lose my shit on them about that later.

The bathroom was all black and wood as well. The shower was huge and had jets coming out on all sides. It was literally the best shower of my entire life. If it wasn't for the whole being held against my will thing, I could've easily gotten used to this type of life. When I dried off, I threw on an oversized shirt and gently ran a comb through my hair.

God, I looked rough. I had a handprint on my throat, scrapes across my face from where I fell, and red rings around my wrists. My blue eyes looked bloodshot and beyond tired. Although, considering it was well past three in the morning, I wasn't surprised.

"You're going to have to wear clothes around the house." I jumped and whacked my hip against the vanity.

"Fuck's sake. You need a damn bell around your neck." I rubbed my hip bone. "Another bruise to add to the list."

Tristan ignored me and sat the tray of pizza down on the bed and licked my legs with his gaze. "You can't walk around wearing a shirt and nothing else in a house full of men. Especially a house with Sebastian in it. He will lose his shit." He stalked towards me, and I backed up until my back hit the shower. He just smiled like something I had done was humorous before digging through the drawers. "Here," he said. "Give me your wrists."

I stepped closer and reluctantly gave him my hands. His tattooed fingers rubbed the cream into my sore skin. The relief was instant. I didn't realize how badly they had been stinging until then. His hand then found my chin and pushed it up to expose my neck. Out of habit, I pushed my chin back down, conscious of the jagged scar there. I hated that I was self-conscious of it. It was proof I had survived, but it was also a link to my past. And it reminded me of it every time I saw it.

"Fine," he sighed and sat the cream down on the sink. "Put that on your neck. It'll help with the pain."

"Thanks."

"Get a good night's sleep, Scarlet." I followed him out and watched him go. Well, I watched his ass go. "Oh, and there's a fan for noise in the back of the closet. We knew you wouldn't be able to sleep without it." I shot my eyes up to his face, hoping he hadn't caught me gawking. I felt my cheeks flush.

He just winked and shut the door behind him. And then I heard the lock click. I figured that was coming.

After I ate every single slice of pizza he brought me and drank the entire bottle of water, I found the fan and turned it on. I really didn't want to know how they knew that little fun fact about me. I had never been able to sleep in silence. Ever since I was a little girl, I had slept with a fan to help drown out the noise of my parents fighting, and it was a habit that had followed me into adulthood.

Lying down on the bed, I passed out before my head even hit the pillow.

CHAPTER
four

SCARLET

The dreams were back. Scratch that. The nightmares were back. I really shouldn't have been surprised seeing as I had been safe for three years and was then suddenly thrown right back into the world that I'd run from. Right back into the world where someone tried to kill me.

In my family, when you turned twenty-one, you inherited your money. Your trust fund, if you will. And not only did you get your trust fund, you started to get jobs. Don't get me wrong, you learned at a young age what it was to be a part of an organized crime family. You learned that violence was always the answer. You learned to keep your mouth shut. And you learned to cover up your illegal money with legal businesses.

But when you turned twenty-one, the responsibilities kicked in. You got your own business to run, your own stocks to take care of, and you were let in to the world in a way you hadn't been allowed to be previously. At least that's how it was with the Dalcas. My fucked-up family. And on the night of my twenty-first birthday, someone tried to kill me. But the thing is, it wasn't some outside attack like we were always expecting, always waiting for. This one had to be an inside job because it happened in my own damn house.

My family's mansion. The mansion that was heavily guarded at all times by men with assault rifles, years of training, and a supposed loyalty to the Dalca family. But whoever it was that snuck into my room that night was met with a woman who had been trained just as hard as the men. I fought that asshole the entire time. But when I felt the blade slice across my throat, I swore that was going to be the end.

I could still remember the feeling of blood oozing over my fingers as I fell to my bedroom floor. I figured I would lie there and bleed out, or he'd finish the job quickly to shut me up. But he knelt beside me and looked me in the eyes. God, I would never forget his eyes. His entire face was covered in a ski mask, but those fucking eyes stared me down.

"I think I'd like to sample the goods before your body gets cold," they said in a whisper. "And scream all you want, baby. No one is here to save you. I like it when my women fight me."

Adrenaline flooded my body as he grabbed onto my pajama shorts and ripped them off my body in one hard tug that burned my skin. My jaw bled freely as I used every ounce of strength I had left to fight him off. He underestimated how small I was, and I was able to turn over in his grasp and get a good right hook in. He stumbled back just enough that I freed a leg and kicked him hard in the crotch.

He doubled over on the carpet, and I ran to my window, my hands shaking from a fear I had never felt before. Hot tears were falling down my cheeks, mixing with the blood on my neck. I had screamed plenty in those few minutes we were fighting, and no one had come running. I was unguarded. I had to get out.

"Fuck, fuck, fuck, come on!" Finally, I got the window unlocked and climbed out of it, holding on to the ledge with my hands and stretching my body out to lessen the fall from the second story. I landed in the bushes and rolled to the cold ground. The wind was knocked out of me, and my entire body was screaming from the impact. But I knew I had to get to the garage and get a car and get the fuck out of that house.

I ran through the slick grass, half-naked and barefoot. I couldn't stop crying, but I also couldn't stop running. There was no room for weakness in this world, and I was losing too much blood. I needed to get a car and get to a hospital and then get the hell out of this city before they could find me and finish the job. I took the first car I could find the keys to and sped the entire way to the hospital, crying and clutching my neck.

"Stay alive, bitch. Stay alive." I blasted the music and had the air on cold, full blast. I just had to make it to the hospital. When I finally arrived, I stumbled in through the emergency room and left the car in the garage. My family was so wealthy, they wouldn't even miss it. I stole some clothes from the lost and found and snuck out once the doctors had stitched me up. If I had stayed any longer, someone would've reported the incident, and they could've found me.

Never leave a trail. The family motto. So I snuck out into the night and made a plan.

I had made it for three years. Three whole years of working four different jobs just to survive. Three years of living in shitty apartments with shittier roommates. But at least it was my life I had made for myself, and no one was lurking in the corners trying to kill me. Three whole years of pure and blissful peace.

So when I woke up in the unfamiliar mansion, throat raw from screaming, and violently punching what felt like a brick wall, I was instantly transported back there. Back to that night with a man on top of me, ripping my pants off.

"Scarlet Izabela Dulca! Wake the fuck up!"

My eyes flew open and met angry dark ones. Sebastian. He was on top of my hips, his hands trying to hold my arms to the mattress, and his hair was mussed from sleep. And probably from fighting me.

"Get the fuck off of me!" I shouted loud enough to wake the dead. Sebastian's hands flew up in surrender as he rolled off me and sat on the other side of the bed. I was trying to get my breathing under control because I was going to hyperventilate if I didn't calm the fuck down. My entire body was frozen in place. I had to tell myself I was fine. There was no one trying to rape me. There was no one trying to kill me.

"Pet?" Sebastian's voice was a little more than a whisper. He reached out slowly to place his hand in mine. I squeezed it so hard I thought I might break his bones, but he didn't even flinch.

"I'm sorry if I punched you," I said through gritted teeth. "You didn't deserve it this time."

He laughed and lay down next to me, still letting me crush his hand. The mattress shifted as he curled up next to me, his bare chest brushing against my arm before tossing one of his legs over mine. The pressure across my body was calming.

"It's okay. Little pain never hurt anyone."

I felt his smile even though I couldn't bring myself to look at him just yet. I had worked so hard to not be afraid of my nightmares, to not be ashamed of what happened to me. His other hand came up to my face and he trailed his finger lightly over the scar. I flinched but let him continue. "Who did that to you, little one?"

"Someone that definitely didn't get what they deserved."

"Mm," he murmured, taking my jaw in his hand and running his thumb along the jagged line instead. He nuzzled his face into my hair. "I can remedy that." I took a deep breath. "Do you want to hear what I would do to them, princess?" Before I could stop myself, I gave a slight nod. Despite myself, I was curious as to what his particular brand of torture would be.

"Yes," I whispered.

"I would cut off each and every finger that touched you, knuckle by knuckle." His breath was hot against my ear as he took it between his teeth. "I would string them up and cut them all over their body just as they cut you. I would cauterize each wound so that they didn't bleed out and die too quickly. I like to play with my food." I squeezed my thighs together at the ache growing there. His hand traveled down my throat and danced along the tattoos across my chest. "I would let you watch," he said as he licked my scar.

God, this should really not be doing things to my body.

"I thought Tristan told you I was off-limits," I said, finally turning to look at him. His hand stilled, and he looked at me with a small smile. We were so close, our noses could touch if either one of us moved the slightest amount. I chewed on my tongue piercing to keep myself from doing anything stupid. His hand came back up to rest around my neck, squeezing gently.

"Tristan doesn't control me, pet. I always get what I want."

I was having trouble controlling my breathing. My nipples were straining against the fabric at my chest, and my core was pulsing with need. My lips parted slightly as I tried to get ahold of myself, and he reached out and grabbed my bottom lip with his teeth. "But not tonight," he said as he let it pop out of his mouth.

I looked back up towards the ceiling, breathing heavily. I knew he could sense how turned on I was. It didn't take a genius to see the way my body was responding to his and to the violence he promised. He kissed the side of my head.

"You can sleep now, little one." He rolled off the bed and jumped onto his feet. "Sleep well knowing I will personally castrate anyone who tries to put their filthy hands on you." And with that, he was out the door, locking it quickly behind him.

    I looked at the clock next to the bed. 5:00 a.m. It really shouldn't have, but knowing Sebastian was close enough to hear me have a nightmare calmed my nerves. I ignored the painful ache between my legs and rolled over, pulling the covers completely over my head. I really needed to have a serious discussion with my body. These men had just taken me from my perfectly safe life not even a few hours ago and planned to sell me back to the family that made me this way. And here I was panting like a sex-starved teenager.

    I was not brought here for a fuckfest vacation, and I would not let myself get sucked back into this life. I had to figure out how to get out of this place before I wound up back in the hands of someone who wanted me dead. Whoever that was.

    I swore and punched the mattress a few times before rolling back over on my back and running my hands over my face. I tried to get comfortable and control my breathing. Count to five on the inhale, count to five on the exhale. I let my mind go absolutely blank. I didn't want to lie around and worry about what was going to happen later that day, later in the week, whenever it was they were going to sell me off.

    And there was no way I would be able to get all the shit done I needed to running on an hour and a half of sleep. I needed to be well rested and in my right mind to be able to get myself out of this situation. I needed to learn my way around this place, listen in on any and all conversations I could, and try to get them to trust me.

Them trusting me was going to be paramount to me getting the fuck out. If they kept me locked up in this room all day, every day, I would be a sitting duck. I let myself run through all the possibilities of escape. My mind went over so many different scenarios I started to lose track. Eventually, my breathing started to even out, and my eyes drifted shut.

CHAPTER *five*

SCARLET

I stretched my arms above my head and rolled over, coming face-to-face with blond hair and green eyes.

"Good morning!"

I rolled my eyes and groaned. "You're far too chipper. Also, why the fuck are you in my bed?" I ran my hands down over my face.

"Oh, is Sebastian the only one allowed to grace your bed?" I turned my face towards him, trying to keep my cheeks from burning, but his smile told me he saw it anyway. Tristan let out a deep chuckle and rolled off the bed. "Get dressed." He had on a white T-shirt and tight black jeans that hung low on his hips.

"Casual today?" I asked as I rolled out of bed and went into the bathroom to brush my teeth.

"It's just you and me for the rest of the morning,"

he called from the bedroom. "I had to send the boys out on some errands in the city. Figured I'd give you a tour around the house and grounds."

I finished and came out tearing a brush through my hair. "You're going to show your prisoner around her prison?" I searched through the drawers and pulled out a bra, a pair of panties, and a pair of black ripped jeans.

"You're such a pessimist."

I scoffed and turned around to put my bottoms on. He got a clear view of my ass as I pulled the lacy thong up into place with a soft snap. But I wasn't about to go change in the bathroom when he was the one in *my* room. The jeans were my favorite pair and fit over me like a second skin. I walked over to the closet, keeping my back to him, and tossed the shirt on the floor while I hooked the bra.

"Is it cold outside?"

He laughed under his breath and picked the shirt up off the floor and laid it on the bed. "Yeah, it's definitely winter in England, Scarlet. Wear a sweater."

I threw on a baggy black sweater and went back to the bathroom to french braid my hair on either side and throw on some makeup. I knew I wasn't going to be seeing anyone except them and maybe the staff, but I was in the habit of hiding my scar as best as I could. It wasn't that I was vain, I just didn't want to be reminded of my past every time I caught a glimpse of myself in the mirror.

When I was done, I walked back out into the

bedroom, and he had lain back down on the bed, his feet dangling off at the knees.

"Can we get some breakfast first? And please tell me you guys keep coffee in this place?"

He sat up on his elbows and smirked. Fuck, I wanted to kiss that stupid look off his face.

Smack. I wanted to smack that stupid look off his face.

"Of course we do." He stood up to his full height and slung his arm around my shoulders. "Let's go get our girl some coffee, shall we?"

The walk to the kitchen was a long one. Tristan said the original kitchen in the house was converted into a large commercial-type kitchen for parties and, shockingly, weddings that they rented the place out for in the spring and summer. There was a smaller, more modern one a little bit further down the hall where everyday food was kept. It had large windows against one wall and french doors in the middle that led out onto a sprawling patio overlooking the back gardens.

Tristan motioned for me to sit down at the bar and made his way over to a very fancy-looking coffee maker that I would have had no idea how to work. I was sure we had one similar at my old house, but I had grown up being waited on hand and foot and never needed to work in the kitchen. Yes, that makes me sound spoiled, but truth is, I was. And when you grow up like that, you don't really see anything wrong with it. Then, when I left and had to make it on my own, I burnt everything I tried to cook for months before I finally got the hang of it.

"Cream and sugar or black?" he asked, pulling me out of my thoughts.

"Black, exactly like my tainted soul, please."

"Pancakes alright with you?"

I leaned forward on the counter and gave him a look. "You can cook?"

He rolled his eyes at me and started digging through the refrigerator. I watched the muscles in his back work as he lifted all the ingredients out and sat them on the counter.

"We didn't grow up with a silver spoon in our mouths like you did, Scarlet. We had to work to get to where we are."

"Work. Interesting word for blackmail and brute force."

"Oh, because your family did everything by the book?" I shrugged. The smell of coffee filled the air, and I turned my attention back out of the windows while he got to work. After the pancakes were cooking, he sat a cup of coffee in front of me and sipped on his own. He had put a ton of sugar and cream in his own which I scrunched my nose at.

"You completely cover up the taste of the coffee that way, you know."

He ignored me. "So," he said with a pause. I looked up at him. "What's the story with the badass scar?"

I sighed and sat my coffee down. I didn't like talking about what happened, but part of me wondered if I told them if it would garner me any sympathy. If they knew what I had gone through at the hands of my family, would they let me go? Chances were slim, and I didn't really want to get into it with a complete stranger. At least not the part about the attempted rape. That part would stay with me, for now.

"Someone tried to kill me."

He looked at me for a moment before flipping the pancakes. He turned back to me and crossed his arms, making the muscles on his tattooed biceps stand out even more. "When? Who?"

"The night I ran away. And I don't know."

He nodded once and then stacked some pancakes on a plate and sat them down in front of me with some butter and syrup. They smelled so good my mouth started to water. I slathered them in butter and syrup before taking a huge bite.

I closed my eyes and sighed at how good they were. I hadn't had real, edible, home-cooked food in years. Yes, I did learn how not to burn my food when I cooked it, but that didn't mean it tasted any better. If I didn't cook, I was getting takeout. Home-cooked just hit different. A small moan escaped my lips, and when I opened my eyes, Tristan was staring at my mouth. I licked my lips.

"What? Do I have syrup on my face?" I asked through a full mouth. I swallowed and wiped at my face but didn't feel anything. He took another drink of coffee and started putting his own plate together, completely ignoring my question. *Whatever.* I went back to shoving bite after bite into my mouth until they were completely gone and I was pregnant with twin food babies.

"I've never seen someone so small eat so much," he

said as he downed the rest of his coffee. I shrugged and looked at him across the counter.

"So, what's the plan, Tristan? I'm here in this really, really nice house, you're cooking me breakfast and taking me on tours of the grounds. What's your grand scheme? Where does selling me back to my family come into play here?"

"That's on a need-to-know basis, and you, Scarlet, do not need to know." He picked our plates up and put them in the sink.

"You're such an asshole. I may not need to know, but I sure as hell would like to. It's my future, my life. Did you ever think maybe I left for a damn good reason? Did you ever think that maybe you're going to try and sell me back to people who don't want me? Or maybe they want me dead? Hell, they may just tell you to kill me yourself. Then what?"

"Why would your own family want you dead, Scarlet?" He leaned back against the counter again, arms crossed.

"I don't know." I tugged on the ends of my braids and stared off behind him at nothing, zoning out. "I don't know who it was that tried to kill me, but I do know it had to be an inside job. It was done in my house, in my bedroom, and I screamed. God, did I scream. But no one came for me." My eyes found his. "No one, in a mansion filled with family and guards, came running to help the supposed heir to the Dalca throne."

"Well, someone definitely stands to gain something with you out of the picture, then."

"No, shit, Sherlock."

"Any ideas who that might be?"

"Nope," I said and sat my empty coffee cup back down. "And seeing as you three aren't doing anything to help me—quite the opposite really—let's stop shooting the shit and get this tour over with so I can stop looking at your pretty face." And the second that was out of my mouth, I bit down on my tongue. He smiled wide, showing off those perfectly white teeth.

"You think I'm pretty, Scarlet? I'm flattered."

I rolled my eyes and jumped down off the barstool. "Don't let it go to your head, pretty boy." He didn't move, just kept staring and smiling at me. "Well? Lead the way," I said, gesturing out the door.

He led me to the front of the house, digging out some heavy coats from the closet and throwing one at me.

"Put that on." I shoved my arms through it and watched him dig through the wellies. "Here," he said as he handed me some knee-high ones. "These are your size. It's going to be muddy out there." After we had put our boots on, he put on his own jacket, zipped it up, and then zipped up mine. He pulled my braids out from the jacket and gave them each a tug. I grabbed his wrists and pushed him away.

"Do not pull my hair. We are not in primary school, and I don't like you." He laughed and threw his arm around my shoulders again and led me out through the front door.

"I could pull your hair like we're in bed," he said as he grabbed both braids in one hand and yanked my head back. His face was inches from mine, and my entire body was pressed up against the side of his. Heat spread through my belly.

"I will never go to bed with you," I said once I could find my words. One side of his mouth pulled up, and he let go of my hair. But I couldn't seem to stop staring at him. His arm tightened around my shoulders again.

"Keep telling yourself that, Scar," he said, trailing his fingers across the scar on my jaw. The new nickname didn't sit right.

"Do not call me Scar. I do not need a nickname that reminds me of the ugly mark on my face."

His eyebrows pulled together, and he dropped his hand from my face. "Your scar isn't ugly, Scarlet. It's beautiful. It's powerful. It's a mark of survival, not of weakness. So when I call you Scar, it's a fucking compliment. Take it as such."

I opened and shut my mouth a few times, not really knowing how to respond to that. I had tried for years to not be ashamed of what had happened to me, but not once had I ever told myself my scar was beautiful. And neither had anyone else.

"Let's go," he said and started pulling us out to a barn off the side of the property.

He unlocked and pulled open the heavy doors and walked over to one of the many quad bikes parked inside. With a turn of the key, the thing roared to life under him. He patted the seat as I made my way over to him.

"Do I not get my own?" I said loudly over the noise of the engine.

"And give you a chance to run away? Never, princess. Hop on and hold on." I sighed but swung my leg over the seat and scooted up next to him. "Hold on," he said again as he revved the engine. I groaned but wrapped my arms around his torso. His rock-hard torso that I could feel even through the thick material of his coat. He reached back and grabbed my hips, pulling me flush against him.

"Much better."

The ghosts of his fingertips lingered on my hips as I held on tighter than I needed to.

Yeah, I thought as we pulled out of the barn, this was going to be a very long day.

CHAPTER

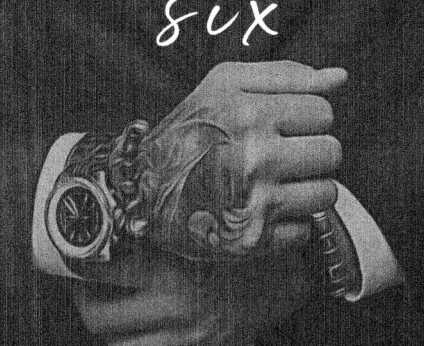

six

TRISTAN

That was the longest morning of my life. I dropped Scarlet and her constant questions off in the den with a babysitter to watch TV while I went to find the boys for a debrief on their morning events. I could still feel her thighs pushing into my hips and the soft curve of her tits on my back. She was big fucking trouble in a small package. I needed her out of this house and back with her family before she got under our skin.

The moment I had found out that she was in my city, I knew it was the perfect opportunity to grab her family by the balls. I couldn't imagine how she thought it was smart to hide just one city over, but that wasn't really my concern at the moment. My main concern was getting her family under our thumb. I wanted them to leave us and our city the fuck alone from now on.

"How was everyone this morning?" I asked as I walked into my office. The guys were both sitting on the couch, drinking from my personal stash. I sat down across from them.

"No issues," Elliot said. "All the businesses paid their taxes and thanked us on our way out." The taxes we collected were separated from anything government required. Our taxes were collected to keep our men on those businesses, making sure they weren't fucked with by anyone else.

"How was your morning with our princess?" Sebastian was already too attached to the pretty little thing, and I really, really should've seen that coming. He may be the enforcer in the group, but he was also the neediest. The most affection starved.

"She's fine. I took her on one of the quads earlier around the property to get her out of the house for a bit. Garret is babysitting her in the den right now." Sebastian stood and started to walk out. "Where do you think you're going?"

"To babysit our girl," he said like it was the most obvious thing in the world.

"We have shit to discuss, Seb. Sit the fuck down. You can kiss the ground she walks on later." My god, Elliot was a grumpy bastard. Turning his attention to me, Elliot raised his eyebrows in a question. "What's the plan for her? When can we get rid of her?"

Sebastian whined like a petulant child at that. I sighed.

"We need to go about this carefully. I don't want to throw it in their faces. That'll just piss them off." Sebastian fell back onto the couch in a huff. "And I don't care about money…and she does not need to know that." I gave them both a pointed look. "For all I care, she can think all she is to me is a way to make few quid. But this whole thing is about getting them to leave us the fuck alone."

"Some serious shit went down with her," Sebastian chimed in. "You didn't see her last night. She was fucking terrified. You really want to send her back into that?"

Elliot groaned. "Seb, how exactly is that our problem? You literally torture and kill people on a whim, but you're worried about sending the girl back to her family?"

"She told me today she's pretty sure it was her family that put a hit out on her. It happened in her room, and no one came for her even though she was screaming bloody murder. And with a family like that, you know there had to be guards everywhere. So—" I took a breath. "—I believe that much."

"They did more than try to kill her." Sebastian chewed on the sides of his nails.

"How do you know that?" Elliot scoffed.

"I could tell by the way she reacted when I was on top of her trying to get her to wake up. And she flinched when I touched her." He stared Elliot down for a minute. "They had their fucking hands on her."

"And why the fuck do you care, Seb? You haven't even tasted her and you're already whipped." Elliot loved to push his buttons and knew exactly what to say to do it. Sebastian's eyes flared with anger. We were minutes away from me having to break up a fistfight.

"Alright, enough, the both of you." I sighed and ran my hands over my face. "Jesus Christ, who knew that that little piece of hellfire would be so complicated."

"Me. I did." Elliot was looking smug.

"Why don't we just use her as leverage instead of handing her back over and trusting them to keep their word?"

"What kind of leverage?" I asked. He just smiled. "You mean keep her, don't you?" He nodded.

"Think about it. If they truly wanted her dead, we would be doing them a favor by keeping her. We keep her a secret, just between them and us. Their family gets to do whatever the fuck they wanted to do without her, push whoever they want to the forefront of the family. All the while we keep her here, keep her safe, and keep them in line. Because if they overstep, we've got her in our back pocket to shake their shit up."

I could practically feel the heat coming off Elliot. This was the last thing he wanted. He hadn't even been completely sold on the idea to go get her. But Sebastian had a good point.

"Sebastian, you may actually be onto something there. That might be a better idea than just handing her over and taking their word that they'll behave. I don't think your little pet is going to like that idea though."

He just smiled and stood up off the couch again. "My pet," he laughed and started to move out of the room. "She's all of ours. Just give it a little more time. She'll have all of our dicks wrapped around her pretty little fingers."

Elliot let out a loud laugh at that and threw his drink back in one gulp.

I watched Sebastian walk out of the office. His words hit a little too close to home. I could still feel the ghost of her body pressed up against my own. And that mouth. Fuck me, the mouth she had on her. She didn't take any of our shit, and I could only talk sense into my cock for so long.

"Not you too," Eliot groaned, pulling me out of my thoughts.

"You can't tell me she isn't sexy as hell."

"Her mouth ruins it."

I groaned, thinking about how good that mouth would look around my cock. "Her mouth most certainly does not ruin it."

He rolled his eyes and sat his glass down on the stand next to him. I took the opportunity to adjust myself.

"We have the party tomorrow night. What are we going to do with her?"

I had completely forgotten about that party. There was definitely no cancelling on something that important. It was a night for all the people who ran the city. Well, the figureheads we allowed to mimic running the city. They were all in our pockets, and they would expect us to show our faces.

I thought about how good she would look on my arm in a sexy little dress, her black hair around her shoulders, tattoos on display. She'd knock all of them on their asses and make all their wives green with envy. That could be entertaining.

"We'll take her."

"We'll what?"

I cringed at how his voice reverberated around the room. "Keep your fucking voice down, Elliot. You're like a brother to me, but I'm not going to sit here and let you yell at me or question my decisions."

"We make decisions as a fucking team, not as a dictatorship."

"Fine," I said because he had a point. "We'll vote on it."

"Fuck," he groaned and stood. "I know what Seb's answer is, so fine. We take her. But I want to go on record saying if this blows up in our faces, this was not my idea and I was against it."

"Yeah, yeah," I said as he made his way out of the office. Probably off to work out. He was the bulkiest out of all three of us just because he had anger issues and liked to work his shit out on the weights instead of people. Maybe Scarlet could help him with that issue as well. I dug my phone out of my pocket and dialed.

"How can I help?" Emily was one of our personal assistants, and I figured she'd be the most qualified for the job of getting Scarlet dressed for the party.

"Emily, we are out at the Wheaton Estate for the foreseeable future, and I need you to get some things for us."

"Go ahead."

"I need you to bring a good selection of women's

clothing for the event at the nightclub tomorrow, size eight. Shoes, UK size five. We will also need most of our wardrobe brought here—we really only keep enough here for a long weekend."

"Yes, sir. Anything else?"

"Not at the moment. Thank you, Emily." I hung up the phone and made my way out to where I'd left Scarlet and found her asleep on the couch, snoring. Sebastian rubbed her feet while *John Wick* played on the TV. Seb looked up and gave me a shit-eating grin. A pang of jealousy cut me through the chest, and I forced it back down. The last thing we needed to be doing was fighting over a piece of ass.

"She's coming with us to the party tomorrow," I said quietly enough that it wouldn't wake her. "Emily is bringing her a selection of clothes and bringing the rest of our stuff out here. I'm going to arrange for someone to stock the food."

"You really think it's a good idea to bring Emily out here to dress another woman?" He was referring to our past with Emily and how she had made her way through all of us at one point. But that was ancient history, and she was damn good at her job. I shrugged.

"Emily isn't on the menu anymore. We don't shit where we eat, remember?"

"Oh, I fully remember. And I don't want her anyway. But that doesn't mean she isn't going to get jealous as shit when she sees her."

"Fine. Keep an eye on her while she's here. No one fucks with Scarlet."

He continued to work her feet but smiled slowly. He could look sinister as fuck when he wanted to.

"Trust me, no one is laying a finger on her."

With that, I walked off to make some more phone calls. If we were going to try and keep her, we needed to be prepared to stay out here for a while. At least until we could trust her. God knew how long that was going to take.

CHAPTER
seven

SCARLET

I lay on my bed and watched Emily roll in rack after rack of clothes. They had brought multiple cars just to fit everyone's stuff in one go. The guys were also very particular about their clothing, it seemed. Emily watched me out of the corner of her eyes constantly. I just smirked and hopped off the bed when I saw a red silk number get rolled in.

I pulled it off the rack before she could pull it the rest of the way into the room. It had the thinnest spaghetti straps, a very low square neck, and a slit on one side that would go all the way up to my hip. It was going to hug every single one of my curves and leave very little to the imagination. I wouldn't be able to wear anything underneath it, which would hopefully prove to be distracting to the boys. Well, for at least two of them.

I hadn't been able to afford clothes this nice for years, and it felt amazing to run my hands all over the nice fabrics. I knew the guys were going to look sharp as hell for the party, and I was determined to outshine them. Emily watched me from the corner of the room as I held the dress up to myself in the mirror and appreciated the shiny, smooth fabric.

"I'll wear this one tonight," I said out loud to no one in particular. I didn't know why, but Emily's presence bugged the shit out of me, and I had been practically ignoring her the entire time. I was never a huge fan of girls as friends. They were too bitchy, too bratty. And Emily looked like a Grade A Bitch. Kenna's friendship had been a rare occurrence.

I sighed. Kenna. I really needed to talk to the guys and see if they could make sure she knew I was okay. I knew Kenna, and she would most definitely have been freaking out ever since I was taken. I needed to let her know I was okay and get her to move on and keep her nose out of this world.

"And the rest?" Emily asked, sounding incredibly bored. "Anything else that catches your eye?" She leaned up against the wall and watched me with her arms crossed.

"All of them."

Her eyes almost flew out of her head, and she choked back a cough. "All of them?"

I looked around. There had to be at least a hundred thousand dollars in clothes and shoes in the room. And that didn't include all of the jewelry and lingerie she had already put in my closet.

"Problem?" I asked her as I hung the dress up on the back of my closet door. If these guys were going to hold me against my will, I was sure as hell not going to take it easy on their wallets. And who knew how long I had left alive if they were about to ship me back.

"You cannot possibly need all of these clothes. This is a ridiculous amount of money, and there is no way the boys are going to be okay with you spending this much."

The boys, huh? Interesting that she was on such relaxed terms with them. I looked over at her, and I could see the jealousy flush across her skin. *Oh*, I thought to myself. *That's why the bitch has been side-eyeing me.* She had most definitely fucked at least one of them, if not all of them.

"Call them, then," I said on a sigh as I fell back on the bed.

"Listen, bitch," she whispered but was promptly cut off.

"Call who, princess?" Sebastian asked as he appeared at the door like I had summoned him.

"Seb, she wants all the clothes," Emily said, swaying her hips as she advanced towards him across the room. An anger I didn't know I could possibly feel roared to life in my stomach. He flicked his eyes from me to her and then back to me like he couldn't stand to look at anyone but me. The heat from my anger quickly turned into a different kind of heat. "There's no way Tristan will want this girl," she spat out, "to spend that much of your money."

Her hand slithered up the side of his bare bicep, and that small amount of her skin touching his set my nerves on fire. My eyes had been locked on his but flickered to her touch for a brief moment. Long enough that he saw it and smiled. In the blink of an eye, he had her hand in his, twisting it behind her back at a painful angle. She cried out, and I sat up a bit straighter.

He kept his darkened eyes on mine while he spoke low in her ear. I licked my lips.

"I am going to tell you this once, and only once, Emily. And if you want to keep your job, you'll listen. My little pet gets what she wants, no matter what it costs. You don't question her. Ever. And if you want to keep your life, keep your fucking hands to yourself. I never want to feel your hands on my body again, or I will break them."

I rubbed my legs together at the warmth pooling at my core. His eyes lazily dragged down my body and landed on my thighs as they moved against each other. She whimpered against his grip.

He pushed her away and told her to get out. I'd never seen someone run out of a room so quickly.

"Someone likes nice things," he said as he adjusted himself and walked over to the racks, browsing through all the clothes I had kept.

"If you guys are going to keep me here against my will, I may as well have a little fun." I watched him from the bed as his eyes found the bright red dress I had chosen for the party. His grin was absolutely feral as he looked back at me. I swear to god, the room got fifty degrees hotter with that look.

"Seb," Elliot said from the door, completely breaking the tension that had been building like a popped balloon.

"Hey there, Grumpy," I said sweetly, pulling his attention to me instead. He looked over with a pained face. He was looking extra godlike in his sweaty gym clothes and his hair tied up in a bun.

"Emily left here in quite the rush. Seemed a little upset. Any idea what happened there?"

I played with my nails like they were the most interesting thing in the world. "No clue," I said on a sigh and looked to Sebastian. "Any clue what was wrong with Emily, Seb?"

He flopped down beside me on the bed and smiled wide at the use of his nickname. "Not a clue, doll." His fingers danced along my bare thighs.

"Not a clue," I said with a shrug, looking back at Elliot. He pinched the bridge of his nose and took a couple of deep breaths. The grey sweatpants he was wearing were doing wonders for him down south. I bit my lip, and Sebastian surprised me by pulling it out with his thumb, his eyes hooded with lust.

"Hands. Off." Elliot's voice was deep and angry, but Sebastian just laughed and gave me a quick kiss on the lips before bounding off the bed. I stared after him in shock. He turned around at the door and winked before disappearing and leaving me alone with Elliot. "I don't know what game you're playing. But leave them the fuck alone."

I stood up and walked over to him, getting close enough I could feel the heat coming off him. His breathing became shallow, and the already impressive bulge his sweatpants weren't hiding very well started to grow. I leaned into him, pressing my chest against the hard plane of his stomach and wrapping my arms around his waist. Fuck, he was tall.

"I'm not playing at anything, handsome," I said sweetly. Both of his hands gripped around my neck with some serious strength and held me in place. His face came so close to mine I could feel his breath play across my lips. His now very hard cock was pressed against my stomach. I was already wet for him, my pussy throbbing at the thought of him just taking me up against the wall. I groaned. It had been too long since I'd gotten laid, and their anger and violence called to me in a way I couldn't help.

"Unlike the other two, I have the ability to not think with my dick, little girl." He squeezed for emphasis, and I pushed my hips into his. My eyes rolled back at the pleasure that small amount of contact gave me. He hissed through his teeth. "My cock may want to punish you until you're screaming my name through grunts of pain and pleasure, but I'm smarter than that." He released me, and I stumbled back in shock before the anger took over.

"You aren't going to treat me like a piece of trash, Elliot." I got back up in his space and pushed against his chest. Even though he didn't budge, it still felt good to do. "I didn't ask to be here. If you didn't want me around, you should've just left me alone!" I gave him another shove, and he just smirked.

"We leave in two hours. Get showered and dressed and be ready when we come for you." With that, he shut the door behind him, and I heard the lock slide into place.

"Phrasing!" I yelled through the door. I gave a short snort at my own joke before turning around to admire all the newly acquired clothes. I wondered if they'd let me keep them all when they got rid of me.

I turned on the shower as hot as I could possibly get it and stepped into the stream. I closed my eyes and ran my hands over my body. These boys were driving my body insane. My nipples went hard under my touch. Fuck, I was going to have to take care of this so that I could get my head on straight.

One hand played with my nipples while the other grabbed the detachable showerhead and flicked it over to the pulsating setting. Really, you put a girl in a room with a detachable showerhead, what the fuck do you expect her to do? I leaned my forehead against the cool tiles as my pussy clenched in anticipation. I imagined Sebastian's fingers on my nipples, Tristan's mouth on my clit, and Elliot's strong hands around my throat.

The water found my little bundle of nerves, and I cried out before covering my mouth with my hand. I groaned at the intense pleasure already coursing through my belly. This wasn't going to take any time at all; they had me so wound up. Sebastian's mouth closed around one of my nipples in my mind, and I moaned again.

Elliot's hands tightened around my throat to where I could barely breathe, his stiff cock teasing me as it moved against my ass. I pressed the water closer as I imagined Tristan's tongue flicking my clit and then moving inside of me like I was the best thing he had ever tasted.

All three of them, worshipping my body like I was the only air they needed to breathe. The warmth built and built inside of me, my toes curling and my breaths coming hot and fast. Somewhere in the back of my mind, I knew I was being too loud. My moans were that of a sex-starved woman on the brink, and I couldn't help myself. As I crested and flew over the edge, I screamed and fell down to my knees, my walls clenching around nothing but air as I imagined riding Tristan's fingers. I dropped the showerhead, too sensitive now to feel it against my skin.

I took a moment on the shower floor to collect myself and catch my breath. Once my legs felt steady enough to stand on, I put the shower back together and took my time exfoliating, shaving, and conditioning. If I was to be arm candy, I was damn sure going to look, smell, and taste the part. They had the shower stocked with anything a girl could need in all different delicious scents.

It took me the rest of the time to do my hair in soft waves and my makeup dark and heavy as per usual. I sniffed through the assorted expensive perfumes they had left for me and dabbed it behind my ears and on my wrists. The silk of the dress sat against my smooth skin like it was made especially for me. The fabric dipped low at my breasts, and the slit stopped just at the crook of my hip. The hem hit just below my knees, and just as I got my heels on, Tristan unlocked the door and made his way in—without knocking again.

"Would it kill you to knock?"

He was dressed head to toe in black. That suit fit him like a glove. I could see every defined muscle. He had his rings on those tattooed fingers, and his neck tattoos stood out nicely against the black collar of his shirt. This guy was sex on a stick. He had his white-blond hair pushed back out of his eyes, showing off every hard angle of his handsome face.

His eyes raked across my body, and when his mouth curled up in a smirk, it took me right back to what I had imagined it would feel like on my cunt. I felt the heat spread through my belly and across my chest. He advanced on me, and for a moment, I thought maybe my fantasy was about to play out. Instead, he held out a black diamond choker.

"May I?"

I nodded as he moved behind me. I held my hair up, and his fingers brushed my skin as his clasped the necklace against my throat.

"How was your shower, Scar?" His breath was hot against my ear. "Eventful?" I could practically hear the smile in his voice. He had fucking heard me. I knew I had been too loud.

Instead of letting myself be embarrassed, I turned to face him and smiled as I grabbed ahold of his belt loops and pulled him closer to me.

"It was a lovely shower, thank you for asking. I especially like the detachable showerhead feature."

He groaned, and his head fell back as he rubbed his hands over his face. "You're killing me."

I laughed and walked over towards the door. "Let's go, handsome. The big guy promised hell if I kept him waiting."

CHAPTER
eight

SEBASTIAN

I made sure to be hot on her heels as she climbed into the limo. God, her ass was perfect. If that dress was any tighter, it would rip right off her. It clung to every single inch of her luscious curves, and it was all I could do to not throw her over my shoulder and take her upstairs to fuck her senseless. Whatever that material was, she would be wearing it from now on.

I practically dove into the seat next to her, and her bright red lips quirked up to the side as she took me in. My hand found her thigh and squeezed the flesh there as Tristan settled on her other side. Elliot was the only one of us so far that didn't seem to feel the gravitational pull she had around her.

"So, who gets the job of babysitting me tonight?" she asked.

I felt rage flow through me. I had told Tristan I wanted it to be me. It's not that I didn't trust Elliot, but I didn't want to be separated from her. I wanted to have my eye on her at all times. She was not getting away from us tonight. Elliot opened his suit jacket, showing off the multiple guns he had strapped to him. A cruel smile spread across his face. She groaned, and that noise went straight to my cock.

"Sebastian trusts you far too much, and you would just distract him," Tristan answered. I squeezed her thigh and let my hand wander a little higher up that slit in her dress. Christ, it went all the way up to that sweet dip in her hip. She couldn't be wearing anything under that dress. My dick stirred again, and I not so discreetly adjusted myself. "And I have too many people to speak with to carry you around on my arm all night."

Even though she tried to look over at Elliot with tough, no-bullshit eyes, I could see the unease slip into them. She was afraid of him, and rightfully so. We were all fit, but Elliot took it to the next level. The guy was an absolute beast and didn't take any shit from anyone. And my little pet was still on his shit list. Well, maybe our little pet. Tristan seemed to be getting a bit cozier with her as well.

She was eerily calm the entire drive to the club. The only thing to tell me she was alive was how her breath hitched every time my hand squeezed her thigh or slid a bit further up that opening in her dress. I wanted to take one of my knives out and slice right up through the rest of that dress and watch it fall off her.

She looked up at me as we pulled up to the club and smiled like she could read my mind.

"What you're thinking is written all over your face," she said, her mouth an inch away from mine, and then she followed Tristan and Elliot out of the window.

Fucking tease.

Tristan and Elliot walked in front, leading us up to the bouncer, leaving me to follow behind Scarlet and thank Christ because her ass was sculpted just for me. Watching it move under that dress and not being able to touch it was going to be fucking hell the rest of the night. She turned around and winked at me before swinging her hips a bit more as she grabbed Elliot's arm and marched right in like she owned the place.

The club was much darker than we had expected it to be. This was more of a rave and less of a "business" party. I pushed up closer to Scarlet and gripped the back of her neck. She leaned back into it without hesitation like it was a subconscious reaction.

"I'm not leaving her in here with only one of us to keep an eye on her," I said into Tristan's ear. "Since when did this little soiree turn into a rave?"

"I know. The plan has clearly changed. We all stay with her. It's too easy for her to slip off in a place like this." He said it loud enough over the music for Elliot and Scarlet to hear. She just rolled her eyes and let go of Elliot's arm and moved closer to me. My hand left her neck, and my arm fell across her shoulders. "I don't like this. We can't keep an eye on our surroundings. Elliot, call some of the guys that are nearby and tell them to come over here. I want extra eyes."

"Can we at least get me a drink?" Scarlet asked over the music.

"Seb and I will take her up to our table. Get your ass up there as soon as you're done making the calls."

Elliot nodded, and we walked our way through the crowd to the upper level. My hand moved back to Scarlet's neck, effectively keeping her on a short leash, and Tristan was holding her hand. Both of us, it seemed, wanted to keep a hand on her at all times. I smiled to myself.

I was sure Tristan was worried she would get away and cause him to miss out on the deal with her family, but I just wasn't done being around her yet, looking at her, touching her. Even her scent was intoxicating.

Tristan took one step off the stairs and stopped dead in his tracks, causing Scarlet to slam into the back of him. I was instantly at his side, blocking Scarlet from view as five rival gang members stood up from our table. They had a fucking death wish being on our side of town, our club, and at our table.

Ty, one of the higher-ups, stepped forward, his gold tooth shining as he smiled past us, finding Scarlet. My blood boiled, and my fingers itched to throw one of my knives straight into one of his eyes just for fucking looking at her. She grabbed the back of my jacket and tried to look around us, but neither one of us moved.

"What are you doing here, Ty?"

"We heard you had a new plaything," he all but shouted over the music. Scarlet's hand clenched tighter. "Thought we'd come see if the rumors were true. If you actually found her. Let's get a look at her, then."

"Over your dead fucking body will you ever get to look her over like a piece of meat." It shouldn't have come out of my mouth. But it did. I would skin all five of them alive before they got to ogle our girl. I felt Tristan stiffen to my right.

"She's not here to be the entertainment, boys. We are here to do business, and you aren't welcome. You need to get out of this club now before it becomes a problem."

I saw Tristan move his hand to the gun at his hip, and I moved in sync with him. Wherever Elliot was, he needed to make his way up the stairs quickly.

They all moved in unison towards us, or towards the stairs, I really couldn't tell. Tristan and I pushed Scarlet over to the side of the staircase, caging her in between our backs and the wall behind her.

"Can someone explain what the fuck is going on?" Not surprisingly, her voice came out much stronger than it should have. She should have been terrified. But there she was, trying to squeeze out from behind us to get a better look at the situation.

"Would you stop?" Tristan scolded her over his shoulder. If I had to guess, her face probably turned bright red with embarrassment and anger at the way he had just spoken to her. I almost laughed out loud at the image of her pouting behind us.

They made their way over, and Ty got up in Tristan's face and smiled. He peered over his shoulder at Scarlet, who, once again, should've been cowering behind us but instead stood there with her arms crossed, examining her nails like she couldn't give two whole fucks about the whole interaction.

I felt Elliot come up beside us, towering over all five of the guys like the damn grim reaper. The tension in that moment was enough to even set me a bit on edge. My body was humming, ready for the fight, begging for it. It had been so long since I had had a proper fight. And showing off in front of my pet wouldn't be the worst thing.

"Wanna come away with us, love? Five men fucking you senseless would be so much better than three."

And before I could do it, Scarlet pushed out from behind Tristan's shoulder and clocked Ty right in the fucking face. I laughed out loud and watched as Ty wiped blood from his mouth.

"*Maldita zorra.*"

"Did you just call her a cunt?" I asked.

I saw red.

"Fuck," Elliot groaned from somewhere behind me as I finished the job Scarlet had started. I hit him so hard I saw his gold tooth go flying. Tristan and Elliot jumped into the fray of fists. To my right, Scarlet leaned against the wall and let a laugh fall out of her gorgeous fuckable mouth.

I saw one of Ty's goons grab for his gun, but I was quicker. I aimed and shot right between his eyes just as he was getting ready to point his at Tristan. Screams broke out all around us as the club quickly turned into a madhouse. All three of us had our guns drawn on the last three standing. Ty was still knocked out on the floor, and the other three were bloodied and bruised.

"Enough! Let us get Ty and we'll go, man."

I hummed and looked over my shoulder at Scarlet. She was leaning up against the wall, her eyes bright with excitement. She chewed on her bottom lip and looked up at me. "Do we let them go, pet? You're the one they offended. Your call." I knew I would get shit for that later from Elliot, and maybe even Tristan, but they would never show any disagreements between the three of us in public. And this was the perfect opportunity for her to show them she could be one of us. We could keep her.

Keep her. My mouth watered at the thought.

Scarlet pushed herself off the wall and sauntered over in between me and Tristan. She reached up and grabbed my hand with the gun and slowly pushed it down to point at Ty.

Fuck me, I was going to marry this woman.

"He's the one that called me a cunt and suggested they all fuck me senseless." She looked up at me with those big blue eyes. "Is there someone above him, or is that pitiful asshole the leader of the entire gang?"

"There's plenty above him," Tristan answered for me.

"Then let's shoot him and send him back as a message not to come onto your territory again. And most importantly—" She paused. "Most importantly, this will tell them not to fuck with *me* again."

My cock was going to fucking explode. She pressed her front up against my side and placed her hand over mine. Her finger slid over mine on the trigger. Her tits pressed up against me with each heavy breath. Her face was flushed, and her lips were slightly parted. She was turned on.

"Are you wet, princess?" I whispered so only she could hear. She smiled and licked her lips. That was answer enough for me. I couldn't believe how lucky we were to find this girl whose body purred for violence. "Are we killing him or maiming him?" I asked as we looked over at the other guys practically shitting themselves.

"Bro, come on. Just let us get him and take him home."

That plea fell on deaf ears. Ty was starting to stir on the ground. In her heels, Scarlet was able to almost rest her chin on my shoulder. I looked over, and she smiled. Her other hand wound its way around my neck and pulled me in. She kissed me and pulled my bottom lip between her teeth as she pulled the trigger. Her mouth tasted like candy, and I let my mind wonder what the rest of her would taste like.

"Fuck!" Out of the corner of my eye, I saw them collect Ty's dead body and head down the stairs, leaving the other one I had shot bleeding brain matter on the steps. That was annoying. Leaving us with the cleanup. Scarlet gave me another quick kiss and then peeled herself off me.

"That was fun, boys," she said as she slapped Tristan on the shoulder. She stepped over the guy on the stairs. Like me, they were both staring at her like she had grown another head. Or that she was the sexiest fucking thing we had ever seen in our lives. Even Elliot looked a bit taken with her in that moment. She made her way over to our table and sat down in one of the chairs, throwing back one of the drinks that had been left on the table.

"Looks like the club has cleared out. Does that mean we get to stay and have some fun for ourselves?" She picked up another drink and finished it as well. She looked up at us all and smiled. "We didn't get all dressed up just for some assholes to ruin our night, did we?"

CHAPTER
nine

SCARLET

Should I be freaking out right now? I just fucking shot and killed someone.

    I was sitting at the table throwing back drinks as quickly as they could pour them. The entire club had emptied out except for the bar staff and the backup Elliot had called for. They all stayed downstairs to give us our privacy while the bartender just left us multiple bottles of various liquors to share between us and four glasses. The extra guys had cleaned up the body, and even though there had been exploded brain matter there thirty minutes ago, you wouldn't even know.

    I didn't think I had ever felt so calm in my life. I had been in plenty of fights. And plenty of those had involved guns in my face or knives at my throat. But I had never killed a person before. I didn't know what had come over me. I was turned on, absolutely out of my mind with lust, watching them beat the shit out of those guys just because they had disrespected me. I could still feel the evidence of that lust on my inner thighs. A downside to not wearing any panties.

And when Sebastian looked at me and gave me the choice, I felt liberated. My entire life had been dictated by men in charge. The heads of the family. Even the boys that were younger than me had more of a say over my life until I turned twenty-one. And really, even then I wouldn't have been able to actually call the shots. They would've found a way to put a guy over my head somewhere, regardless if I was my father's only child.

But the assholes that sat across from me, laughing and swapping stories of their first kills, they had given me power. I looked down at Seb's hand resting possessively on my thigh, following the tattooed dotted lines that went all the way to the tips of his fingers. I wondered if I could fit in with them. My family didn't want me alive anyway. So what if they kept me? It would certainly be a way to keep me out of whatever business my family didn't want me a part of. It would be the end of my hiding and running. I could be relatively safe. I could be in one place. I could have a home.

I took a deep breath and threw back another shot. The glass rattled on the table as I sat it down.

"Keep me."

Three pairs of eyes turned towards me as they all shut up at the same time.

"Princess, we already—" Sebastian started, but Tristan held up his hand to stop him.

"I know what you already decided." Tristan quirked his eyebrow. "I know you decided to give me over to them for a ransom, but hear me out, okay?"

Elliot groaned, but Tristan nodded, and I leaned forward, my forearms propping me up slightly on the table.

"I wouldn't be some little thing you needed to protect. I know how to fight. I was trained from a young age how to shoot a gun and use a knife. My hand-to-hand combat might be a little rusty, but I can work on that. Let me earn your trust. Give me a job so I can earn my keep. I'm really smart with computers. Like, really fucking smart. Let me help you guys out in some way. Let me contribute."

"And what about your family?" Tristan interrupted.

I sighed. "They don't want me alive anyway. At least some of them didn't. I don't know why, but they obviously don't want me around. So the only reason they would pay you a ransom would be so that they could kill me themselves. But maybe you could make a deal. Tell them you guys will keep me and that you will keep me out of their way. And as payment for that, they can stay the fuck out of your territory and stop making moves over here."

Sebastian leaned back in his chair and smiled over his glass. I could feel Elliot stewing from where he was, but I knew I'd made some good points. I could see it written all over Tristan's face that he agreed with me.

He played with the rings on his fingers for a moment before meeting my eyes.

"Okay," Tristan said and shrugged. My eyes must've become saucers. I'd expected him to make that much harder.

"Okay?"

He smiled, and Seb squeezed my thigh. I looked around at all three of them. I stood up and shoved my hand out towards Tristan. I was impressed with myself when I saw it wasn't shaking.

"Shake on it," I said. "Shake my hand and tell me you will keep me and won't send me back there. It would be signing my death warrant, and I really, really don't feel like dying." My voice may have wavered a bit at the end, but honestly, whose wouldn't? I was trying to save my life.

"And you don't think staying with us is signing a different type of death warrant?" Elliot chimed in.

"If we keep you, claim you as ours, people on our payroll will leave you alone, but you'll have a different type of target on your back." Seb's hand had fallen from my thigh when I stood up, but it found the crook of my arm while he spoke, like he was trying to make sure I was listening.

"We've never claimed a girl as ours before," Tristan said, leaning in. I dropped my hand and sighed. "We've shared plenty, but we've never offered anyone our protection."

"I'm not asking for protection," I said, ignoring the ugly jealousy that roared through my veins at the mention of them sharing someone else. Emily's pretty face flashed in front of my eyes. "I'm asking to be useful. I'm asking to be a part of something that might actually want me instead of being shipped off to a family that doesn't."

"Well, I don't want you."

I turned towards Elliot and smiled. "Your hard-on when I shot Ty tells a different story, Grumpy."

"Just because I want to fuck you doesn't mean I want to keep you around. You're a whole lot of trouble in a tiny package."

"Hey," Seb said towards Elliot as he pulled me down onto his lap, right onto the massive erection he was sporting. "Don't talk to our girl like that. She's part of the fucked-up family now." He pushed my hair off my shoulder and planted a sweet kiss on my neck.

"Not until we fucking shake on it," I said, shoving my hand towards Tristan again. "Shake on it and promise me you won't send me back there."

Tristan laughed and grabbed my hand. "Fine, poppet. Done deal. You're ours now." A shiver skirted its way down my spine at the look in his eyes.

"Now that that's done, can we please go get some food? I'm starving," Sebastian groaned.

"Oh, yes please. I would love some chips and gravy to soak up this alcohol."

Tristan stood up, buttoning his jacket closed as he took one last shot.

"We've probably been sitting here too long anyway. If they're going to retaliate, they know where we are. So let's get out of here, get some food, and go back to Wheaton." I was absolutely starving. I hadn't eaten anything since lunch, and if I didn't get something in my stomach soon, it was going to empty out all the liquor I had just drank.

We made our way out of the club, the backups following us out the door. Instead of going in the direction of the car, they started walking down towards the group of food trucks in the town centre. The smell was fucking fantastic as we made our way there. There were a few groups of friends in various lines, laughing and chatting away with each other, the alcohol obviously making them numb to the cold.

Sebastian grabbed my hand and took me to the one he claimed had the best chips and gravy out of all of them. I asked them to add cheese and watched in sheer drunken delight as they drenched the entire plate of chips with thick brown gravy and topped it with white shredded cheese. My mouth watered at the savory smell. When Sebastian handed me the steaming plate, I shoveled as many in my mouth as I possibly could.

"Think you'll finish that entire thing? Should I get my own?"

I scowled at him. "Over my dead body will I share my food."

He held his hands up in mock surrender and ordered himself the same thing. Tristan and Elliot walked up with extremely greasy burgers in their hands. I had almost finished my entire plate of chips, but my stomach still growled at the thought of having one of those.

"Oh my god, where did you get those? I want one."

"I just saw you literally destroy an entire plate of

chips and gravy and you want to shove a burger down your throat?"

"Don't shame the girl, Elliot," Tristan said as he waved another burger in front of my face. "I figured you'd want one as soon as you saw we had one. So, being the caring gangster I am, I made sure I got you one."

I shoved the last couple of chips in my face and threw it away before ripping the burger out of Tristan's hand.

"I honestly might bust right the fuck out of this dress if I eat this, but I don't even care. It smells so good."

Elliot rolled his eyes, but Sebastian just laughed and threw his arm around my shoulders.

"None of us, not even Elliot, are going to be angry about that dress falling off your body, babe. And those moans you make when you eat…fuck."

"Let's get back to the car before we get hit by another shitstorm, please," Elliot grumbled, trying to shuffle us all back the way we came. The driver had at least pulled the car a bit closer to where we had wandered off, so I didn't have to walk much further in the heels. The other guys were dismissed by Tristan as we walked up to the car.

"I swear to god I have twin food babies. I think I'm going to explode." I was so full I felt sick. Tristan opened the door for me, and Seb was right behind me, his hands resting around my neck.

"I honestly don't know where you put all the food you eat."

I rubbed my hand over my full belly, letting it stick out and showing off my cute little bump. The satin dress stretched over it way too tightly. I made a note to myself to wear something with a little more give next time. He gave it a soft poke, and I groaned. I needed to get home and get this stupid dress off.

I crouched over and climbed into the car. Seb and Tristan both gave my ass a hard smack, and I heard Elliot sigh.

"You guys are so pussy whipped and you haven't even sampled the goods."

I sat down on the seat, fully prepared to throw a sassy retort in his direction, when the unmistakable sound of fabric ripping filled the silence. I looked down at my dress and saw the slit that had previously stopped at my hip now reached all the way up to the underside of my boob. I looked back up at the guys and saw them all staring at my bare skin, drooling like dogs for a meal.

I started laughing. That uncontrollable belly laugh that takes over your entire body just poured right out of me. Part of it was the alcohol, and the other part of me just found it so fucking funny that the dress had been so tight that I had been able to rip it just from eating. Tears started rolling out of my eyes, and my stomach hurt from laughing so hard. I lay down across the seat, trying and not really succeeding at keeping the dress closed, as Seb shuffled his way in to sit down and lay my head on his lap.

"Someone's got the giggles," he said as he brushed

my hair out of my face. "But I will say I'm a fan of the new look. Much easier access than before."

I grabbed his arm and tucked it under my chin. His hand gripped my shoulder, and I closed my eyes, finally coming down from my fit of giggles. I took a deep breath.

"I killed someone tonight."

I could've cut the tension in the car with a knife at that point. No one said anything, but Seb just kept tracing circles on my shoulder with his thumb.

"If you stick with us, it's not going to be the last time you kill someone." Elliot's deep voice took me by surprise, and I turned to look at him. "You have good aim," he said on a sigh like it physically pained him to compliment me.

"Her hand didn't shake. She didn't hesitate. It was an amazing shot right between his beady eyes," Seb said.

Tristan's eyes were glued back to his phone screen, but he took a second to look up at me and give me a wink. "You did good."

Seb grabbed my jaw and made me face him next. "If you had chosen to just maim the bastard, I wouldn't have let him walk out of that club alive."

"I know, you crazy fuck." I laughed and rested my hand on his arm that I kept tucked beneath my chin.

They started talking amongst themselves, and between the massive amounts of food and the alcohol in my system, the comforting hum of the car began to lull me to sleep. I don't know what it said about me or them that I felt comfortable enough with them to sleep all the time, but I just didn't feel threatened.

Well, maybe a little threatened by Elliot. But the other two were cinnamon rolls. I felt protected and somewhat welcome. Especially after what had gone down in the club. So, I didn't question it. I accepted my circumstances and let myself sleep soundly for the first time since I'd run away from home, knowing no one was going to come and kill me in the middle of the night.

CHAPTER
ten

SCARLET

I felt one of them lift me out of the car and carry me through the door. I was very capable of walking, but killing someone will really take it out of you mentally. So instead of waking up and making whoever it was put me down, I decided to curl into their chest and wrap my arms around their neck. My dress had fallen wide open when he had picked me up, but I was too exhausted to care.

When we finally made it to my bedroom, I lazily opened my eyes and saw it was Sebastian who had carried me upstairs. Not a surprise.

"Hey, beautiful," he murmured into my hair. He laid me down on the bed, and I didn't try to cover myself up as the dress came open. I was still feeling the effects of watching the guys beat the shit out of those other men earlier. Especially Sebastian, who had ultimately given *me* the power. What better way to thank him than to let him get his dick wet? And I was only human. These men were fucking godlike with their tattoos and piercings and muscles for days.

As Seb rooted through my drawers for something resembling pajamas, I lay back on the bed, propped up on my elbows, and brought one leg up to give him a show when he turned around. When he finally did, I was not disappointed. He threw his head back and groaned. I laughed to myself.

"Oh, pet," he said, bringing his eyes back to mine. I just smiled and opened a little wider for him. I was so wet already he could probably see the evidence of it even in the dark.

"I thought maybe you could help me take the edge off?"

He ran his hands through his dark hair and looked at me for a moment, like he was trying to decide how bad of an idea it was. To be honest, it was probably a really bad idea. But god he was fucking beautiful. The tattoos covered every inch of skin I could see; even the ones on his neck went all the way up to his jawline, and they drove my pussy wild.

He slipped out of his jacket a moment later, and I watched as his hands started to unbutton his shirt, revealing the rock-hard abs and delicious vee that slipped underneath his pants. Every part of his torso was covered in the same style of boldly colored tattoos. They disappeared under the waistband of his pants, and even in this dim light, I could see the unmistakable outline of his cock begging to be let out.

He walked over to me and propped a knee up in between my thighs as he bent over me. His body hovered over me, his hands on either side of my head, eyes dark and holding mine. I breathed him in, relishing in the way he smelled like cologne and tequila.

"If we do this, princess, you're going to be mine, and I'm not going to let you go."

I laughed and lay back on the bed as I wrapped my arms around his neck, effectively pulling his entire body on top of mine. "I'm already yours, Seb. I belong to all of you after that deal earlier, remember? So we may as well have some fun while I'm here." I pushed my hips up and ground into him, eliciting a groan from deep in his chest that went straight to my core.

"I am going to fuck you until you come so many times that you'll beg me to stop. And even then, I'm going to continue to fuck you. I am going to fuck you so hard that every time you move tomorrow, you'll remember how it felt to have me inside of you."

Holy shit. I whimpered and pushed my hips into his again. His entire body was flush with mine, and I couldn't get enough of the feel of him.

"I am going to own your body tonight, little pet. This pussy," he said as he cupped me and pressed the heel of his hand onto my throbbing clit. His hand lit my blood on fire, and I groaned as I tried to push into him. His face came closer to mine. "This is mine for the night," he whispered against my lips before dipping a finger into my already slick heat. This time when I moaned, he caught it with his mouth. His kiss was urgent and bruising. It was a war of teeth and tongues.

His mouth trailed across my jaw and down my throat, biting so hard in places I knew he would leave marks. But I liked some pain with my pleasure. He added another finger, and I rotated my hips when his thumb found my clit.

"Fuck, Sebastian, please," I begged, trying to push his head off my nipples and down to where I needed him.

"So responsive," he said after he released my nipple with a pop. "You're soaking wet for me, princess." He withdrew his fingers and brought them to my mouth. "Open." The tone of his voice sent a shiver of lust down my spine. I obeyed and took his fingers in my mouth, licking my own arousal off them with enthusiasm, wanting to please him with every fiber of my being. I never wanted to stop seeing that look of desire on his face. That look was all for me.

He pulled his fingers out of my mouth with a smirk and situated himself between my thighs. His mouth made its way down one thigh, stopping just short of where I needed him most before moving to the other.

"If you keep teasing me, I will kick you the fuck out of my room with blue balls, Sebastian."

He laughed a deep, masculine laugh that did all kinds of things to my body. He grabbed my hips and flipped me over onto my stomach, ripping the rest of the dress off like it was tissue paper. He lifted my hips and immediately buried his face into me. I cried out as he went from biting my clit to licking and sucking and shoving his tongue so deep inside me I thought I would explode.

He dipped fingers back into my cunt, massaging my inner walls while his tongue worked circles around my clit. I pushed my face into the bed and bit hard on the blankets. I was so fucking close to coming on his face when he suddenly withdrew his fingers again. Before I could protest, one of his fingers found my ass and began to push so, so slowly. I pulled away slightly, nervous at the pressure building there. A hard smack came down on my ass, and I yelped into the bed. A whole new wave of heat flooded me at the stinging heat on my ass cheek.

"Stay. Still." He rubbed the area where he had smacked me, soothing the sting. "I told you, princess. This body is mine, and I will take whatever part of you I want." He spit in between my cheeks and rubbed his thumb on my clit, making me push back towards him while he pushed a finger into my tight hole. Part of his finger slipped in as he continued his slow, measured circles on my clit.

I was greedy for him, pushing back on his finger, trying to get more of it inside me. My breaths were coming short and fast. I was gripping the sheets in my fists and between my teeth, moaning through the intense pleasure he was causing. The warmth was building to an unbearable level as he moved his finger and his thumb in even strokes.

"Please, don't stop. Right there," I whispered into the mattress.

"Scarlet." My name rolled off his tongue in the

most delicious way. "Come." The authority in his voice sent a ripple of pleasure through my entire body. I was so close my whole body was vibrating with need. He leaned over me, not breaking his rhythm, and bit my shoulder…hard. "Come for me, pet."

My body shattered, and I vaguely felt myself cry out through the sheer bliss racking my body. He pulled his finger out of me and began to lick long, soft strokes from my clit all the way up, while I tried to come back down to earth and regain some sense of self.

"You taste like fucking heaven, pet. Next time I want you to sit on my face and come in my mouth so I don't miss a drop." He blew cool air on my cunt, and I moaned as I tried to push back into his face again. "But right now, babe," he said as I felt the bed shift and heard the sound of his pants dropping to the floor, "I need to be inside of you."

I propped myself up on my elbows and looked back at him as he stripped himself bare for me. *Fuck me.* Even his legs were covered in tattoos. He peeled off his tight black boxers, and I gasped at the sight of him. I couldn't help myself. He was unfairly blessed in both length and girth, and that silver piercing right under the tip of him had my pussy clenching in anticipation.

He stared at me for a long moment, rubbing himself from base to tip. I could see the bead of precum, and my mouth longed to lick it off. I wanted to taste him, feel him quiver and stiffen when my tongue piercing roamed across his flesh. I started to move to do just that when he laid a firm hand on my hip.

"Roll over." I smiled to myself. My sweet, sadistic

cinnamon roll wanted me to play submissive. Fueled purely by lust at that point, I rolled over immediately and looked up at him. "I want to see the look on your face when I'm inside you for the first time."

"Confident it'll be a look of pure bliss and not disappointment?" I may have wanted to please him, but I never said I wouldn't be a brat.

He smiled down at me, a dark smile that reminded me of how an animal looks at its prey, and grabbed my jaw, his fingers digging into my cheeks painfully. I whimpered. What the fuck was wrong with me that this was what turned me on? He gripped it harder, forcing my jaw to move and my mouth to open. He leaned closer and spit right into my mouth.

My cunt convulsed, and heat flared through my abdomen. He loosened his grip on my jaw just enough to let me close my mouth, and I eagerly swallowed.

"Good girl," he purred into my ear as his hand lowered itself around my throat instead. He squeezed and slowly slid himself into me, stretching me to the point I was worried he wasn't actually going to fit. That cold metal of his piercing rubbed against me in the most amazing way. His eyes never left mine, greedily lapping up my every reaction. It was agonizingly slow the way he filled and stretched me. One of his arms snaked around my hips and lifted them slightly so that he could fit his entire length inside of me.

"That's not a look of disappointment," he said as he smiled against my mouth. I opened mine to him and let his tongue flick over my piercing. He began to move with a slow and gentle rhythm as he claimed me with his mouth. He tasted like me and sin, and I soaked up every bit of it. I wrapped my legs around his waist and pulled my hips up to grind on him as he filled me up over and over again.

"I thought you were going to fuck me until I couldn't walk?"

With another wicked grin, he pulled completely out of me, teasing my entrance with the tip of his cock. He ran his piercing over my clit, and another moan escaped me. He sat back on his heels and with a swift jerk, pulled me towards him and wrapped my legs around his waist. In one rough motion, he was back inside me at an angle that made me see God.

I cried out, and he covered my mouth with his hand so roughly I could taste blood, but I reveled in it. I wanted it harder, faster, rougher, and he was willing to do all of those things. He fucked me mercilessly. My body was already begging for another release. When he used his other hand to pinch my clit, I screamed into his palm and rode each wave that passed through my body. He didn't slow down or ease up; instead, he just fucked me at the same pace, still rubbing soft circles with his thumb.

I was too sensitive—it was too much. It was all I could do to hold on to his waist with my legs as he drove his cock into me over and over again. My eyes rolled back in my head as another climax found me, pushing me violently off the edge of the waterfall. He slowed down his thrusts as I twitched and whimpered beneath him. His hand left my mouth and trailed down my chest, tweaking each nipple and twisting until he got a gasp out of me.

"You are the most beautiful fucking creature I have ever seen." He pulled out of me and flipped me over onto my belly. I was a warm pile of goo to do with what he wanted. He smacked my ass again and then kneaded it roughly with both hands. I lifted my hips and pushed back, seeking him out, obviously a glutton for punishment. He laughed spread my cheeks apart as he slid back into me.

"I have an IUD," I said. I looked back over my shoulder at him. "I want to feel you come inside of me."

"Fuck, babe," he said between thrusts. "You want me to come inside you, pet?" I nodded. "Say it. Beg me for it." He picked up his speed, driving me into the mattress.

"Please, Seb," I begged. I didn't care how pathetic it might sound. I needed this man. I needed to feel him claim me. "Come inside of me, please. I need to feel you spill yourself inside of me, marking me as yours. Please."

He grabbed a fistful of my hair and yanked back hard, giving him a better angle. He smacked my ass again, and the pressure started to build. I fed off this tortuous mixture of pain and pleasure.

The tip of his thumb found my ass and pushed in swiftly. Between the sudden intrusion of pain and the fullness I felt, I came again, squeezing his cock for all it was worth. He sped up through my orgasm and then stilled, fully sheathed inside of me as I felt him spill into me. I squeezed him and rotated my hips, milking him for all he was worth. He trailed kisses down my spine and slowly pulled out.

"Stay there, love. Let me clean you up." He came back with a warm, wet cloth and gently cleaned me before helping me into an oversized shirt he had found in a drawer. He pulled down the covers and helped me inside. He kissed me again, softly this time, and then murmured into my hair how beautiful I was.

"Stay with me," I said through a yawn.

He did.

CHAPTER
eleven

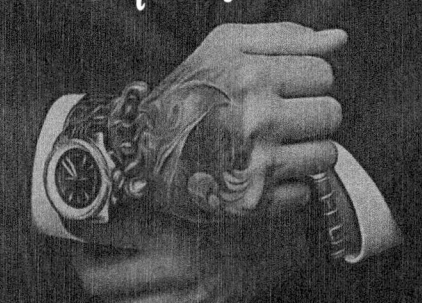

SCARLET

Sebastian held true to his word. We had sex three more times that night, and by the end, I was begging him to stop. I had never had that many orgasms within that short of a time frame, and I was pretty sure my pussy was going to short-circuit. When I woke up, it was with a hangover and a very sore body. Sebastian's arm was draped across my torso, and his breathing was even.

 I slipped out from under him and threw on a T-shirt before sneaking out of the room and down to the kitchen. Every step was a bit painful, sending very clear memories of all the incredible sex I had had in the last few hours. Sebastian was right—I would be remembering what he felt like all day. I remembered the way to the kitchen pretty easily, and lucky me, sitting at the table was Elliot, looking like a tatted Li Shang with that man bun and those muscles. He was, of course, shirtless because all of these guys seemed to like to torture me.

"Good morning, sunshine!"

He looked up at my cheery greeting and raised his eyebrows as he took in my bare legs. "Sounded like you and Sebastian had a fun night last night." I made my way to the pantry and rooted around until I found the sugariest cereal they had. "Judging by the bruises, I'd say you're feeling a little sore."

"You," I said, pointing the box of cereal in his direction as I made my way to the fridge to get the milk, "just sound jealous." He scoffed and went back to reading the newspaper. "Who even reads the newspaper anymore? I thought only middle-aged dads sat around in the morning reading the sports section."

He ignored me, so I continued to make my bowl of cereal. I jumped up onto the counter and watched him read while I ate. I looked over at the microwave. 10:00 a.m. I couldn't remember the last time I had been able to sleep that late.

"Hey, where's Tristan?"

"Why?"

"Because I want to talk to him about my role."

Elliot sighed and laid his paper down on the table, crossing his arms. "Get your dirty, bare ass off our clean counter and maybe I'll tell you."

"It's not dirty," I said as I hopped off and put my bowl in the sink. "Sebastian took very good care cleaning me up last night." I winked at him and got an eye roll in return.

"He's in the music room," he said as he picked back up his paper.

"There's a music room?"

He threw his head back and rubbed his eyes. "You are fucking insufferable. Yes, there is a music room. There are many rooms. It's on the other side of the house, ground floor, back right-hand side. Just keep following the hallways and you'll eventually hear him drumming away in there. Now please, leave me alone."

I held up my hands in mock surrender and made my way out of the kitchen.

It wasn't as hard to make my way around the house as I thought it would be. Since I was pointed in the general direction, it only took me a couple of minutes to find him. The closer I got, the louder the drumming became. I had no clue that Tristan was a drummer, and I couldn't tell if he was good or not because honestly all drummers just sounded like they were banging on shit.

But when I opened the door a crack and saw him shirtless, his blond hair flying in all different directions as he twirled the drumsticks and beat the shit out of those drums, I decided it didn't really matter if he was any good. Because he looked damn good doing it.

I opened the door the rest of the way and walked in, taking a look around. There were soundproofing squares scattered around all the walls, comfy couches and bean bag chairs, and all different kinds of instruments dotted around the room. He looked up at me and smirked as I took a seat in one of the bean bag chairs relatively close to his drum set. He stopped and turned towards me, twirling and tossing the drumsticks around in his hands like a nervous habit.

"What can I help you with today, Scarlet?" He was out of breath, his muscled chest moving with the effort. I gave him a long look before answering, my eyes snagging on the bars in his nipples.

"I was wondering if I could be put to work soon? I'm going to get bored around here if all there is to do is watch TV."

"It's kind of cute that you think I would trust you so soon to access our private files."

I groaned and rolled my eyes. "What am I going to do with all your precious files? It's not like I have anyone to sell that shit to." He just gave me a pointed look. "Fine. I get it. First thing on the list: earn your trust. What am I supposed to do until then?" He smiled and rolled one of the drumsticks between his knuckles. It made me very curious as to what those fingers could do elsewhere.

"I was thinking we could get your fighting skills back up to par. Elliot is a great trainer. I'm sure he'll whip you into shape quite quickly."

"Oh, fuck me, Tristan," I groaned.

"I think you need a break after Seb, babe. Maybe next time." He winked at me, and I flipped him off even though my very sore pussy clenched at the thought. She needed to calm down and take a breather before trying to convince me to jump right back into bed with one, if not all three, of these guys.

"Turn of phrase, asshole. Sorry if I'm not super stoked to be training with the big guy. He's really not that fond of me, and I'm pretty sure he is going to love beating the crap out of me on the mat."

Tristan laughed and stood to hover over me. He held out his hand and helped me up off the chair.

"Let's go, little Scar," he said as he ran a finger across the scar on my jaw. "Let's go find him and show you where the gym is. After you train with him for a bit, we can have lunch and then take you outside to have some target practice. You'll be happy to hear that will be Seb. We're all a good shot, but Seb takes the cake. He's an excellent marksman."

"And you're just too busy running all your 'businesses' to help little ole me, right?"

"Right," he laughed.

Tristan didn't let go of my hand as we wandered the hallways, him pointing out different rooms as we made our way back to the front of the house. He sent me off to change while he fetched Elliot. I figured with all the clothes they had brought from my old place, they had grabbed everything, including all my workout gear. Sebastian was nowhere to be found when I got back to my room, so I quickly got changed, threw my hair up in a bun, and made my way back downstairs.

"Let's go, Elliot. Time to get this little thing back in shape," Tristan said as he took my hand again. Elliot followed the movement and rubbed his hands over his face. I was very positive Elliot was about to take out a lot of frustrations on me. This was not going to be pleasant.

"I would like to point out that I am not out of shape," I said as we walked off. "I am just out of practice. There's a difference. I continued to work out while I was on the run."

"Compared to what I'm about to put you through," Elliot said as he opened the door to a very impressive in-home gym, "you are out of shape."

I stepped inside and looked around. One wall was made entirely of mirrors with free weights lined up along one side. There were a couple of ellipticals and treadmills, a rowing machine, and a squat rack. Elliot stepped onto the mats in the middle of the room and beckoned me over. Tristan dropped my hand and gave my ass a smack.

"Knock him dead, kid. I've got some business to attend to. I'll come back and get you."

"When?" I asked, glancing over at the clock on the wall.

"Aw," Elliot cooed from across the room. "I think she's afraid to be alone with me, T."

"Never," I said before reaching up and smacking Tristan with a bruising kiss, forcing his mouth to open to mine. He leaned into it, and I took his lip between my teeth and bit hard before breaking it and looking back at Elliot. "I just wanted to know when Tristan would be back, is all." If he had been a cartoon, smoke would've been blowing out of his ears.

"Okay then," Tristan said with a clap of his hands. I looked over my shoulder and smiled at him. "Have fun, you two." With that, the door clicked shut behind him, and Elliot pointed to the mat.

"Get over here and stretch."

I gave him a smirk but did as he said. He went over

to the stereo system on the wall and "Coming Undone" by Korn began to blare through the speakers. Elliot watched me as I stretched for the next few minutes, and I felt my body heat under his gaze. The guy was going to have to stop looking at me like that, or there was going to be more than just training done on this mat.

"Alright then, spitfire. Let's see what you've got. I'll take it easy on you."

"How noble of you."

———

He did not take it easy on me. My bruises got bruises. Every inch of my body had taken a beating. I was kicked, punched, slapped, and tripped eight million different times in the span of two hours. When Tristan made his way back around noon, I collapsed onto the floor in the most dramatic fashion I could muster.

"Okay," I said in between breaths. "Maybe, just maybe, I am a bit out of shape."

"You think?" Elliot asked at the same time that Tristan laughed and helped me up.

"Why don't you go get cleaned up, and I'll make us some lunch before our resident sniper takes you outside for target practice."

I nodded and limped off to the bedroom. A shower had never felt so good. After I was clean, I inspected my bruises that had popped up over my ribs, hip, thighs, and even the vague outline of a hand across my neck. I was covered in brushstrokes of purple and yellow.

I changed into some jeans and a T-shirt before making my way back down to the kitchen. All three boys were scattered around the kitchen. Tristan was cooking, Sebastian was reclined at the table, and Elliot stood at the island, typing away on his laptop. Sebastian patted his legs, and I took up residence on his lap.

"How was training, pet?"

"I think she almost died," Tristan said from the stove. "When I went back to get her, she very dramatically fell to the floor in a heap."

"Big guy over there put me through the wringer with no regard to how tired and sore I already was."

Sebastian tightened his grip around my waist. "Want me to kick him in the dick for you?" he murmured in my ear just loud enough Elliot could hear. Elliot scoffed, but I could tell by the tone of Seb's voice he would actually do it if I wanted him to. I smiled and leaned back into his chest, very content with knowing I had at least one person on my side. I looked over at Tristan, and he was smirking to himself while he flipped the sandwich in the skillet. Well, maybe I had two.

"No, babe. If anyone is going to take him down, it'll be me."

After we ate, me sitting in Sebastian's lap the entire time because he refused to let me go, we made our way outside to the shooting range they had set up in the back gardens. Tristan stayed with me this time, but Elliot had mumbled about having work to do and stomped off with his laptop under his arm.

"Don't take him too seriously," Sebastian said as we

made our way outside. "He's gone through some real shit in his life, and it makes him a lot less trusting than me and Tristan. Give him time. You're one of us now," he said, sliding his arm across my shoulders. "You wouldn't even dream of betraying us, would you?" There was something laced around the edges of his tone that normally wasn't there, and it sent a shiver down my spine. It reminded me that Sebastian might act like the Pillsbury Doughboy, but he was actually a gangster and a murderer. And I'd do well to remember that.

I smiled up at him and shook my head. "Never, my sweet cinnamon roll boy."

Tristan let out a loud laugh and caught an angry glare from Seb. "Cinnamon roll boy," Tristan said, cracking another smile. "Best fucking thing I've ever heard someone call you, Seb. Best fucking thing."

"Only our girl can call me that. Don't get any ideas, T." Tristan just shoved his hands in his pockets and grinned.

Sebastian was loaded down with guns, and I slipped my hand over the shotgun and took it off his arm and slinked out of his grasp.

"I'm starting with this one. I love how these bullets explode. Much less chance of survival." I looked at it appreciatively, and then Tristan slid his arm around my shoulders and pulled me close.

"Yeah, I think you're going to fit in just fine."

CHAPTER
twelve

ELLIOT

It had been one very long week since Scarlet took over the damn house. She pranced around like she owned the place in long T-shirts that barely covered her ass and nothing else. Sebastian followed her around the house with his eyes like a lost puppy. Tristan was barely any better, but at least he hadn't stuck his dick in her…yet.

Every time she came into the room, a smile on her face and a bowl of cereal in her hands, her eyes would flit to each one of us as she smirked and decided which one she would sit next to. It was like she had us in rotation, and every time it was my turn to have her attention, I would just grit my teeth and try my best to ignore how she smelled like lilacs and petrol. She was constantly driving around the grounds on the quad bikes, and that scent followed her around for the rest of the day.

It's not that I had anything against Scarlet herself or that I wasn't attracted to her. But that girl was gunpowder and lead, and I was just waiting for her to get under all of our skin and then blow up in our faces.

We were in Tristan's office, and she was still asleep. That girl would sleep for the entire day if we'd let her. Then again, with Sebastian in her bed every fucking night, she probably needed it.

"Elliot," Tristan said, bringing me back to the room.

"Yeah?"

"We need to make a move with her family. We need to decide how we are going to handle this."

I sighed and ran my hands over my face. "Are we sure we want to keep her around instead of just giving her over as a way to keep their fingers out of our pies?"

"Hah! Phrasing," Seb laughed. I rolled my eyes.

"Honestly," Tristan said, leaning forward on his forearms, "I think it's the best way to guarantee they'll stay under our thumb. It's like having a permanent hostage. A constant bargaining chip in our hands. They'll know if they fuck up we can just use her."

"Fine. How do you want to do it, then?"

"Let's set up a meeting."

"They're going to want proof we have her," Seb chimed in.

"So, we take her with us," I said, leaning back into my chair.

"No way are we taking her and putting her right in

the line of fire," Seb said, his hackles instantly raising. Protective bastard. Tristan sighed and shook his head.

"I agree with Seb. Taking her would give them the perfect chance to just shoot her on the spot. Or take her. We are going to have to leave her here with some of our most trusted people. We can give them proof in the form of a live video feed or something."

I groaned inwardly. I didn't really see this plan working. I didn't trust her. I didn't trust anyone other than the two guys in front of me. And the fact that they had let her in so quickly worried the shit out of me.

We had known her for less than forty-eight hours before Sebastian was fucking her and Tristan had welcomed her in as a part of our circle. Granted, he hadn't let her start working on anything that would give her any ammunition against us, but he was having her train with me every day. He was letting her become more of a threat.

And every time she sauntered into the gym in her sports bra and biker shorts, I damn near lost my mind. I couldn't decide if I wanted to knock her out or throw her on the ground and fuck her into the mat until she was screaming my name. I realized those were drastically different trains of thought, but she seemed to bring out the worst in me, and I wasn't quite sure why that was yet.

"I'll get in contact with them today to try and figure out when is a good time to sit down and talk this out like adults. I want to get Scarlet as comfortable as possible with us, start earning her trust so that she can earn ours." Tristan stood and walked over to his desk.

"Interesting way to look at it." I earned a couple of hard glares at that. "Look, I know I'm the odd man out here. You guys both seem to trust her to a certain extent, and you trusted her pretty quickly."

"I never said I trust her," Tristan cut in.

"I trust her," Seb said. That earned him a look from Tristan.

"You guys literally said yes to her after only knowing her for two days. Don't you think that's a little quick?"

"I was able to build this...whatever this is... on intuition, Elliot. I trust my gut. If I didn't, we wouldn't be where we are today. I'm not saying I trust her, because I don't. I would never trust someone that quickly. But what I saw in her, El..." He shook his head. "She's beaten, bruised, and really fucking down on her luck. Her own fucking family definitely wanted her out of the picture. She just wants a place to belong. Why can't we give her a chance to belong here?"

I sighed and cradled my head in my hands. These idiots were going to be the death of me one day. Tristan hadn't grown up in a happy home. Orphaned at the age of nine, he was thrown into foster home after foster home and never actually had a family until we got together as teenagers. So it came as no surprise that Tristan wanted to pick this girl up as a stray.

I met Tristan in high school. Once we got together, we ran that whole fucking place. We were in charge of the drug trade, we had the best parties, and not a soul made a move without us knowing. He and I were kings of that high school campus. Our operations kept growing as we got older, and once we were eighteen, we decided to start making things look a little more legal.

We had to start explaining where all the money was coming from. Tristan had been the brains behind all of that. He researched and learned how to invest, how to get businesses going, and got people to work for us. Slowly but surely, we started to take the city over, business by business, gang by gang.

There was so much bloodshed in the first few years, I thought we would never wash it completely off our hands. And then Sebastian came into the picture. He was just some kid, fresh out of high school, that waltzed right up to our fucking table one night while Tristan and I were in a meeting. That fucker walked right up to us, ignoring every single gun pointed right at his face, and asked Tristan for a private word.

The balls it took for him to do that immediately impressed both me and Tristan. So when Tristan said yes and paused the meeting, I knew right then and there that that scrawny-looking kid, covered in tattoos, a cigarette hanging out of his mouth like we weren't in a fucking restaurant, was going to be our third.

He had overheard some shit in the car park that turned out to be very useful. After he had divulged that tidbit of information, Tristan didn't even hesitate to offer him a job.

"What can you do?" Tristan had asked him. "What are you good at?"

Sebastian had smiled, and it was ugly and terrifying. It would have a normal person running for the hills.

"I'm a pretty good shot. And I really don't mind getting my hands dirty."

After that, we became the Triad. We had our fingers in everything: clubs, restaurants, drugs, kill for hire, and all kinds of "favors." And we did everything together. All decisions were made with a group vote, never a dictatorship. Until Scarlet. I was okay with being talked into going to get the girl and use her as a way to keep the Romanians out of our shit. But I was a little bit further behind on the bandwagon of keeping her.

When we had come across Sebastian, he had been someone with important information and a very useful skill set. But when it came to Scarlet, she was just a hot piece of ass from a rival family that could supposedly work with computers. And that didn't seem useful to me when we couldn't even trust her enough yet to let her work. So for now, all she was good for was getting Seb's dick wet, tempting Tristan, and annoying the shit out of me.

"Alright," I said, coming out of my own thoughts. "I get it. I trust you, and so I will try to trust her."

"Maybe stop being such an ass to her all the time and she'll show you why I became so fond of her," Seb said, snickering into his coffee.

"Oh, you don't want her all to yourself, Seb?"

"Why would I keep her to myself?" I saw Tristan light up a bit at that. It was a subtle change, but I saw it. "That girl has more to give than one man can handle. And I see the way she looks at all of us. The way she takes turns and makes sure everyone gets attention. You can't tell me you haven't noticed that."

I barked out a laugh because I actually had. I hadn't fully made my mind up as to why I thought she did that, but now my dick really wanted Sebastian's theory to be right.

"Alright, enough," Tristan said. "Go wake her up, El. You were supposed to start training thirty minutes ago."

"Lucky bastard," Seb mumbled. "I want to train our little pet. Rubbing up against her all day. Pinning her to that mat. Slipping those tight short off of her and slipping in..." He trailed off, and I whacked him on the back of the head before making my way across the room.

"Great, Seb. Now that's all I'm going to be able to think about for the next couple hours."

"Good. Maybe getting laid will help that icy exterior of yours." I flipped him off as I made my way out of the office and down the several hallways to her room.

Her room. I rolled my eyes. She had started calling it her room on her first day. Like she had already decided this was also her house. And maybe it was. Maybe having someone like her around to keep Seb in line, give Tristan some consistency and comfort, and give me...I didn't know what she would bring to the table for me yet. But maybe having all of those things wrapped up in a cute little package wouldn't be such a bad idea.

But she still needed to earn my trust. I wasn't going

to walk into this with my cock leading the way. Because if I did, it would blindly lead me straight to her. I opened her door without knocking and found her naked, lying on her stomach with her ass fully on display. Her inky hair spread across the dark sheets.

"Fuck me," I mumbled under my breath.

She turned her head in my direction and lifted her ass, swaying it from side to side, and smiled.

"With pleasure, love."

My cock twitched, and I took a deep breath, letting my icy mask fall back on my face. She was not going to get to me that easily.

"Get up, temptress," I said, leaning against the doorframe. "Time for training."

She smiled wider and lifted her naked body off the bed, shamelessly flaunting every curve of it in front of me. God, her tits were perfect. I didn't let my eyes stray any lower before telling her I'd be in the gym and I expected to see her down there in five. I turned on my heel and stalked out, readjusting myself and trying to think about anything other than her ass in the air.

CHAPTER thirteen

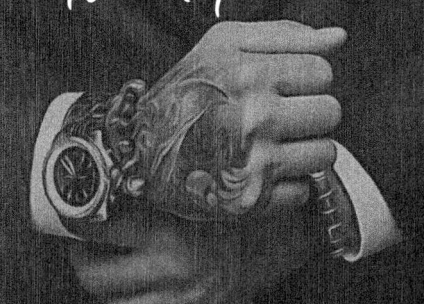

SCARLET

All three guys were on edge, and it was stressing me out. It had been nine days since I was abducted by them, eight days since they told me they'd keep me, and two days since they had called my family and set up a meeting. I was constantly keeping track of every hour and every day they kept me. I couldn't help myself. I woke up every day wondering if they would change their minds. Just because Seb was fucking me and Tristan seemed to be growing fonder of me didn't mean they couldn't change their minds and throw me to the wolves.

Tristan wouldn't tell me anything about anything. He kept telling me it was for my own good. I didn't need to know because I would just worry about it. Little did he know the less I knew, the more I worried. I was completely in the dark on what time the meeting was, where it would be, and what all they would be telling them. The only thing he kept saying was that he promised me he would keep me safe.

Strange words to hear from a leader of a crime syndicate.

Seb had been saying the same thing every night he came to my room. Last night when he showed up, just as I was getting out of the shower and crawling into bed, he had grabbed hold of me with a new force and thrown me onto the mattress so hard I had bounced a few times before he was on top of me, kissing me like his damn life depended on it.

"What's wrong, Seb?" I asked when he had finally released my mouth long enough for me to come up for air.

"Nothing, princess," he had murmured into my neck. "I just need to feel you." And damn did he feel me. He had fucked me into that mattress so hard I saw stars by the time he had finished. When he held me after, tenderly rubbing all the bruises and bite marks he had left, he kissed my hair and murmured, "I will fight anyone tomorrow that tries to tell us we can't keep you."

"It's tomorrow?" I asked.

"Yeah," he said as his hands wove through my hair.

"Feel free to maim or kill anyone you see fit," I said without humor. "I really would prefer to not go back there."

Once the sun was starting to set, they all went to their separate rooms to get ready. I assumed that meant it was time. I snuck into Tristan's room while he was in the shower and made myself comfortable on his bed. His room was the exact opposite of Sebastian's. Where Seb's was dark and moody, Tristan's was bright and almost cozy. Everything about his room welcomed you in. I picked up the drumsticks on his nightstand and tried flipping them between my knuckles like I saw him do so many times.

"You aren't holding them correctly," he said as he stepped out of his bathroom in a burst of steam. His blond hair was still wet, dripping down his neck and the sides of his face. His towel was wrapped around his waist, accenting his delicious muscles. Just like Seb, Tristan's tattoos covered every inch of his rock-hard torso. I didn't think it was possible to have muscles in places where these guys had muscles.

"Whatever," I said, tossing them aside. I was in my usual outfit for lounging around the house which meant I was in a T-shirt and nothing else. When I caught him staring at my bare legs with heat in his eyes, I spread them in a silent invitation just as I had with Sebastian that first time. Maybe I could give him a little more incentive to keep me around. He groaned as he took me in, my sex bare to him. I smiled when I saw his cock push at the towel around his hips.

"Scarlet," he groaned as he sank down onto the bed next to me and caged me in with his arms. I was praying that towel would slip from his hips and I would get a glimpse of him, but that thing had more willpower than Elliot. "I have a very important meeting," he said, moving his mouth closer to mine. I licked my lips, and his eyes followed my tongue with lust.

"I could help you take the edge off." I closed the distance between our mouths, because fuck being the girl that waits for the guy to make the first move, and while he opened his delicious mouth to me, I slid my hand under his towel and pushed it off his waist. He pulled his mouth from mine.

"Scar—" he started, but I took his girth in my hand and squeezed. His eyes glazed over with heat.

"Yes?" I asked him as I stroked him, base to tip, swiping my thumb over the bead of precum. I swiped my tongue across his open mouth, and he moaned. I pushed him back on the bed, and he let me, giving over the power to me. I situated myself between his thighs and admired him, spread out for me like a chiseled god. "Did you want to say something?"

"No."

"Didn't think so."

His cock was beautiful, not as thick as Seb's, but I could still just barely fit my fingers around him. And he was long enough to know that I would be struggling to take him very deep in my throat. My cunt clenched at the thought. I trailed my tongue up the underside of him and swirled it around the head, grazing my teeth just enough to mix a little pain with his pleasure. His abs and cock jumped at the sensation, and I smiled against him.

I took him in my mouth, and he moaned, sending shock waves straight to my core. I loved how in control I felt with a cock in my mouth. He was at my mercy. I was affecting him like this. I had his pleasure in the palm of my hand. His fingers wove themselves into my hair and pushed me further down. I grabbed the base of him, working my hand in time with my mouth. I could hear his breathing change as I felt my own excitement between my thighs.

My other hand snaked between my legs, rubbing circles around my clit. I moaned against his shaft, and he twitched again. I dipped a finger inside myself as Tristan looked down at me, meeting my eyes while I took as much of him in my mouth as I could.

"Fuck, Scar," he whispered as he saw my hand moving between my legs. "Are you touching yourself?" I moaned in confirmation, and that was his undoing. "I'm going to fuck your face now." I grinned and pushed another finger into my cunt as his fingers gripped my hair so tightly tears formed in the corners of my eyes. The pain was exquisite.

He pushed me all the way down on his cock, and I relaxed my throat to take him fully. He held me there for a few seconds, and I swallowed over and over again, enjoying the look of sheer pleasure on his face as my throat moved against him. When he pulled out, I took a breath and let the tears fall down my cheeks. He groaned and pushed me down again, quicker this time, up and down. He pounded into my throat, and I loved every second. The harder he pushed, the faster I rubbed myself.

I could feel the familiar tingle of an orgasm building between my legs at the brutal assault on my mouth. I looked up at him and met his eyes as I fell over the edge of my own orgasm, the most delicious heat flooding my limbs, and he pumped one last time into my mouth. He held me there, spilling into my throat, as I swallowed everything he could give me. He threw his head back and moaned so loudly, I knew the other guys had to have heard it. I withdrew my fingers as he pulled out of me with a *pop*.

I smirked, crawling up his spent body, and lay on top of him. He grabbed both sides of my face in his hands and kissed me hard, licking the roof of my mouth, my teeth, and tangling with my tongue. He wiped the tears off my cheeks when he broke the kiss.

"That was the hottest goddamn thing I've ever seen." I smiled and kissed him again. "You didn't have to do that, Scar," he said against my mouth. "We aren't trading sexual favors for your safety."

I shrugged. "I wanted to." I ran my hand through his still-damp hair. "You've been nice to me when you didn't have to be."

"Sebastian is going to kill me."

I laughed and laid my head on his chest. "No, he isn't. He'll learn how to share." I felt him tense underneath me before he took a breath and started drawing circles on my back with his fingers.

"I need to get dressed." He kissed my hair, and I gently rolled off him, letting him get up and finish getting ready.

"Can you tell me something about how tonight is going to go? Just anything?"

He slipped on a pair of black boxer briefs that

hugged his ass perfectly. "We're meeting them on the border of our territory. At a restaurant."

"Okay," I drawled. "And what's the plan? What are you going to tell them?" He sighed as he pulled on some dark pants and a button-up shirt. He turned around to face me as he rolled up his sleeves, exposing his strong forearms. "Just tell me, Tristan. I don't know what you guys think I would do or could do with any information about what is happening tonight, seeing as I'm going to be heavily guarded by your men and have literally no way of contacting the outside world."

"I'm going to tell them that we found you and are keeping you in exchange for them staying the fuck away from our business. If they want you to stay out of the family business, then we'll keep you out of it. If they fuck with us, we're going to say we will let you loose to claim your title."

"They don't know that I know it was them that put the hit out."

"Yeah, we're counting on that. If they try to play dumb and say that they want you back and they try to pay us off, we'll just tell them we know it was them that tried to have you taken out. So they need to back off or we'll tell them you know it was them and watch all hell break loose." I nodded and leaned back on his pillows.

"You guys need to be careful," I said as I stared at the ceiling. "My father always brings Samuel with him." I took a deep breath, knowing I was about to feed them information that would see me killed twice over if my family found out.

"Who's Samuel? We requested a meeting only with

your father and his second, Mateus."

"Samuel is the guy in the shadows. He will find a vantage point no matter where he is or where you guys are. He's an excellent marksman, would give Seb a run for his money. You would never see it coming. And once my father finds out you have me, he may not hesitate to use him."

Tristan pondered this for a moment before nodding and going back into his bathroom. "Then we'll just have to have our own sniper join us. Make sure the playing field is a little more even."

Sebastian knocked and walked in, looking like the devil himself dressed in all black and covered in tattoos. He looked down at my T-shirt, still bunched up around my hips, and grinned like a wolf.

"Well, well, what happened here?" he asked as he leaned against the doorframe. I smiled and pulled my shirt down as I climbed off the bed.

"Just spreading the love around," I said as I drew up on my tiptoes and kissed him hard on the mouth. His fingertips dug into my hips, and I could already feel his arousal pushing into my belly. Too bad they didn't have time to play. "Be careful," I said as I broke the kiss. "All of you!" I said a little louder so that Tristan could hear from where he was.

"Always, babe," Seb said and smacked my ass as I walked out of Tristan's room and made my way downstairs to the kitchen. If I was going to have to sit in the house, alone all night, worried sick about those idiots, I was going to do it with an ample amount of snacks and liquor.

CHAPTER
fourteen

TRISTAN

"I'll admit, it probably wasn't the best time for it to happen," I said to Seb as we loaded into the blacked-out SUV.

"Best time for what?" Elliot asked as he climbed in after us. Sebastian had been giving me shit for the impromptu blow job the entire walk to the car. "What did I miss?" Elliot had made a last-minute call to get our sniper to the meeting as well, just in case.

"Our boy T here has crossed over to the dark side. He let our little pet wrap that sweet mouth of hers around his dick to take the edge off."

"That was not why I let her do that," I said, firmly cutting him off. But he just snickered to himself and watched Elliot for his reaction. To both of our surprise, Elliot just tipped his head back and laughed. Seb and I exchanged a look and then moved our eyes back to Elliot.

"This girl is going to be the death of us all," he said once he had calmed down. He looked out the window, and we rode in silence the rest of the way there. It was a pretty long drive considering we were on the other side of the city, out in the country, and we had to meet them as close to the border of our territories as possible.

Years of meetings like this had pretty much numbed me to any kind of anxiety or jitters, but this night felt different. We hadn't gone up against a group this established with so much to lose and gain at the same time. If they didn't accept this deal, I wasn't too sure what the next move was going to be.

It had only been a bit over a week since I had met this girl, but I knew we couldn't hand her over to the slaughterhouse. We were going to have to figure out something else to keep her safe if they demanded she be given back.

"Seb," I started as we pulled up to the closed restaurant. "Remember, if they don't agree to this deal, you cannot go into fucking Rambo mode and just shoot everyone up in there, yeah?" His jaw ticked like his body was rejecting the order. But he knew better. He knew we had to tread carefully, or Scarlet could be the one that ended up getting hurt.

He nodded. We all stepped out of the car, straightened our jackets and adjusted our pieces, and walked into that restaurant ready to make a deal for our girl.

Scars

Scarlet's father, who was only ever called *Domnul* Dulca and never by his first name, and his second, Mateus, were already seated at the back of the restaurant. The table was set up so that neither side would face their backs to the front or back of the restaurant. Both of them were seated on their side, and on the other side of the table was only one chair.

To the outside world, I was the leader of the Triad, the one that made all the decisions and ran the businesses. Elliot and Sebastian were seen as my bodyguard and the enforcer, respectively. So when we went to meetings, I sat and they stood. I found out early on in this life that it was good to make people feel off balance. You wanted them a little bit at your mercy. And when I sat down but the two big guys stood behind me, it made them feel intimidated.

"Gentlemen," I said as I pulled my chair out and sat across from them. "Thanks for coming." Scarlet's father was old as dirt itself and severely out of shape. He sat there with his white hair combed over to the side and his belly pushing into the table. His face was passive as he gave me a nod and then looked at the two behind me.

"You said it was important. And I've heard rumors about what this might be about. Let's hear it."

I smiled and leaned back in my chair, comfortable with the fact that if they made a move to use their hidden threat, I could use our own.

"We found your daughter the other night," I said,

folding my hands together on my lap. "At a dirty old house party on the outskirts of our city." I looked at him, but he gave nothing away about how he was feeling. I continued. "Now, growing up in your family, she surely knew she had no business being in our territory."

He grunted and smiled a cold smile that didn't reach his eyes.

"Make your point, mutt."

I felt the guys tense behind me, holding themselves from striking out at them for the derogatory nickname people had taken to calling me…normally behind my back. I wasn't a "pure breed" like these old-timers, and they loved reminding me. Not that it bothered me. I had made this empire for myself instead of just walking into it like these lazy fucks did. I smiled just as coldly right back at him.

"We heard a rumor that she didn't just run away for shits and giggles. Instead, she ran away because someone tried to kill her in the dead of night on her twenty-first birthday. And the specific rumor is that it was you that put the hit out on your own daughter."

He went pale as a damn sheet and coughed to cover up the surprise showing on his face.

"What're you getting at?" Mateus asked.

"We have her. And we're going to keep her. In return for this favor, you are going to keep your greedy little paws out of our business and stay in your own."

"Why would I care if you keep her or give her back?" He scoffed. "She doesn't have the faintest idea who it was that called out that hit on her."

"Because if we give her back, she's going to raise

hell. I will tell her what you did, and she will try to dismantle your entire system. And if you think she won't, then you really don't know her at all. We have known her for a week, and we can already see that she is far more fit to run your little crime organization than you ever were." The words came out of my mouth before I could stop them, but at that point there was no going back. They were out there in the void, and I swore he could see right through me.

"Ah," he said, crossing his arms and leaning back slightly in his chair. "*Deci o fuți pe curva aia?*" *So you're fucking the bitch.*

Pure unadulterated rage flowed through my veins, and it was all I could do to not reach across the table and shove the knife I had tucked up in my sleeve into his fat throat. Out of the corner of my eye, I saw Sebastian move. I may be the only one in our group that understood Romanian, but it was clear in her father's tone he hadn't said anything pretty. Seb just moved an inch before Elliot was able to put a hand on him to stop him, but it was enough for Dulca to notice.

"Oh," he said as his smile grew deeper. "You all are? What a little *curvă* she's become in these past few years." My blood boiled harder than before. If he didn't shut his mouth soon and agree to our terms, we were going to start an all-out gang war with the restaurant being ground zero. "Fine, boy," he said with a wave of his hand. "Keep the bitch. Fuck her, breed her, kill her, I don't care. Just keep her out of our shit, and we will stay out of yours. But first," he said, leaning closer, "I need proof you have her. Not to offend, but I don't trust the words of gangsters."

"Elliot," I said, gesturing for him to give me the phone. "This is a live feed of her in the home where we are keeping her." The screen lit up, and there she was, in one of her Metallica T-shirts, lounging on the couch where we told her to sit until told otherwise and shoveling popcorn into her mouth. It was all I could do to not smile at screen before handing it over to her father. He rolled his eyes.

"And how do I know this is a live feed?"

"Time stamp," Elliot spoke up. "Top right-hand corner." Dulca's eyes drifted towards it and grunted in approval before sliding the phone back across the table.

"Can I ask," I said through gritted teeth, "why is it that you don't want her taking your place?"

"She would've never taken my place. She's a woman," he scoffed like this should've been common sense. Little did he know, I wasn't a bigot. "Besides that, she was headstrong and couldn't take orders. I would've had someone over her head, but she would've never listened. And I wasn't about to let her have access to all the family money."

"You're right. She would've never listened. But that's only because she knows better than you," I said, standing and holding my hand out to him. "Nice doing business with you." He shook my hand without standing. Zero fucking respect for anyone but himself. "If I see or hear of a single one of your guys on our side of things without my permission, I will kill them."

He laughed and pulled his hand from mine. "Yeah,

yeah," he said with another wave of his hand. I fucking hated it when people did that. "I told you we have a deal, so we have a deal, mutt. Just be sure to keep up your side of it. And tell my darling daughter hello for me, will you?"

Seb snorted, and I gave him a sharp look before Elliot led us out of the restaurant.

"That could've gone much worse," Elliot said as we climbed back into the car.

"It was over quickly. Too quickly. He didn't even put up a fight or question us," Seb worried. I agreed with him. That whole meeting went too smoothly.

"Well, for now, we assume he's telling the truth, but be on guard in case he has something up his sleeve. Maybe he does just want her out of their life that badly."

"Badly enough to blindly trust a rival gang to keep her out of it?"

"I'm sure there's more to the story," Elliot said as he put his phone to his ear. "There's no way he was willing to kill off his only kid just because she was a girl. I'm sure that contributed to the decision knowing how he is, but it has to go deeper than that."

"I agree," I said as I scrolled through my own phone, checking emails and making sure I hadn't missed anything important in the last half hour.

"Hey," Elliot said into his phone. "Everything is fine, calm down." He rolled his eyes. "We're done. We'll be home in a bit." He had called Scar? I was shocked, and I knew it was written all over my face just the way it was written all over Seb's. Elliot listened to

Scarlet for a minute and then, "Night," and he hung up.

"Did you just call Scarlet?" Sebastian asked.

"Don't say a fucking word," he said to both of us with that deadly stare I had seen so many people shrink back from. But I just laughed.

"You were worried about her, weren't you?" I asked. "You knew she was worried about how the deal was going to go down tonight, and you didn't want her sitting there freaking out."

"Fuck off."

"Told you," Seb said as he slid down in his seat to get more comfortable. "She's our girl. All of ours."

"Once again," Elliot said, his temper clearly rising. His entire face had gone red. "Fuck. Off."

Seb and I just laughed and went back to scrolling on our own phones, letting Elliot stew in whatever realization he had come to in that meeting.

"He called her a bitch," I said after we had been on the road in silence for some time.

"And a slut," Sebastian pointed out.

I sighed and scrubbed my hands over my face.

"I don't think I have ever been so eager to spill blood than I was in that moment." Seb and Elliot both grunted their agreements.

"I would love to get my hands on him," Sebastian said as he played with the butterfly knife he took with him everywhere. He had that crazed look in his eyes he always got when he was thinking about torturing people. "Maybe one day me and my little pet can slice him up together." He flipped the knife and caught it in the palm of his hand. "She might like to see him bleed."

"She might like to make him bleed," Elliot said, and I snickered a laugh.

How the hell we had managed to stumble across her, a woman that enjoyed bloodshed as much as ourselves, I had no idea. But I wasn't complaining.

CHAPTER
fifteen

SCARLET

I crawled into Tristan's bed after I got off the phone with Elliot and fell asleep pretty much immediately. I had planned to lie there and watch TV or something until they made their way home. I really wanted to ask him how the meeting had gone. Elliot being the one to call had surprised me so much that I had forgotten to ask what had happened. So I just handed the phone back to Matthew, the bodyguard they had put on me for the night, and made my way upstairs.

 I woke up to the weight of the bed shifting and rolled over to see Tristan, naked except for his boxer briefs, crawling under the covers. He snaked his arm around me and pulled me to his chest.

 "How'd it go?"

"A little too easy," he murmured against my hair. "Your dad is a piece of work."

"To put it mildly."

"How did you put up with that for so long?"

"I didn't really have a choice," I sighed. "What was I supposed to do? Run away?" I laughed, and he surprised me by catching it with his mouth. His lips were soft against mine as he stroked my hair. The gentleness of him took my breath away. When he pulled back, he looked into my eyes, and the pity there set off my temper. I sighed and pulled away from him.

"Anything else I should know about the meeting?"

"Whoa," he said, pulling me back into his chest. "Where'd you just go?"

"I don't need your pity, Tristan." It was a look I was all too familiar with. When you run off without a penny to your name, struggle to make ends meet, and constantly look like a starving homeless person, you see a lot of it. "I made my life after him work. I got multiple jobs, made my own money, and had a roof over my head."

"*Scrumpo*," he purred as he gripped my chin. Hearing him call me his precious one in Romanian was enough to thaw my hardened heart. "I was not looking at you with pity. I was looking at you like that because I was sad we didn't get to you sooner. We could've saved you going through all that shit." He pushed my hair out of my face and ran his fingertips down my back. "I see myself in you, Scar. You came from a bad situation, went through hell, and came out of the other end of it alive. And stronger for it." His fingers tangled in the ends of my hair.

I smiled and kissed him again. At a loss for words at how kind he was being, I pushed into him and ground my hips into his. A purely male growl came from his chest as he deepened the kiss and swiped his tongue across my own. His hands drifted down to my ass and squeezed hard enough I knew there'd be little purple bruises across my skin. My hand sought out his cock, but he stopped me, breaking the kiss.

"Scarlet, stop." His hand pushed mine out of the way as his fingers danced around the hem of my T-shirt. "I think I owe you one, love." The tips of his fingers found my bare slit where wetness had already pooled between my thighs. I could've screamed with the urgency I felt to see what those strong fingers could do.

One slowly pushed between my folds and made slow circles around my clit, eliciting a soft gasp from between my lips. I pushed my hips, trying to get him to give me what I wanted, what I needed. I opened my eyes and found him watching me, drinking in every fleeting emotion there. His eye contact turned me on even more and sent a whole new rush of heat through my body.

"Tristan," I pleaded. He just smiled and dipped a single finger inside of my needy cunt, and I clenched around him. It was just enough sensation to send me grinding against his hand. I loved being teased with light touches just as much as being tied up and spanked. His thumb drifted to my clit, and he pushed gently, teasingly, as his finger moved in and out of me with painstaking slowness. My head pushed into his shoulder, and I panted against his bare skin, watching that muscled forearm tense and move against my body.

He pumped another finger inside of me, and I groaned into his shoulder, biting down on the hard flesh there until I tasted blood. He hissed and pushed his thumb in faster circles as he added a third finger. I stifled a scream at how he thrust them deep inside of me, curling them and hitting that spot that made my eyes cross. The steady rhythm he found with those drummer's fingers were about to send me over the edge.

"Do you like that, baby girl?" *God fucking save me.* Baby had never been something I allowed anyone to call me, but coming off his lips, with his hot breath against my ear and his fucking fingers driving me over the cliff, it was the hottest thing I had ever heard.

"Tristan," I moaned against his mouth. I wrapped my hands around his neck, and my fingers tugged on his soft hair.

"Answer me," he said, suddenly slowing his fingers.

"Yes."

"Yes what?" He bit my lip and pulled it into his mouth.

"Yes, sir."

"Good girl," he murmured. "What a good little slut you are. Ride my fingers, baby."

His fingers picked up their pace again as a whole new warmth took over my body at his words. That pressure built, and our breaths mixed. He watched me with hooded eyes as my body relaxed and went taut at the same time. My head lolled back, and I let the orgasm flow through my blood, making my toes curl and my thighs clench against his hand. His name was a whisper on my lips. He saw me through it, his fingers never slowing until I began to twitch, the sensation on my clit too much.

"Fuck, Scar," he said as he slowly withdrew his hand. I took deep breaths and brought my eyes back to his. He brought each one of his fingers to his mouth, one at a time, savoring the taste of me. My hand drifted from his shoulder, down across his hard chest and abs, and began playing with the waistband of his boxers.

"Scarlet," he said, putting a firm hand on mine. "You need sleep. You have training early in the morning." He kissed my forehead. "And I'm not so selfish as to expect something in return every time." He gave me a quick peck on the lips and then pulled me flush against him, cuddling me under his chin. "How is it you manage to still smell like petrol after taking a shower?"

"Do I?" I laughed and tried to smell it on my hair.

"You do. I like it. It's comforting."

"Okay, there's definitely something to unpack there." I trailed kisses up his chest and across his collarbone into the hollow of his throat. It was impossible to be so close to him and not have my mouth on him. "You said you didn't have a great start to life," I said, changing the subject. "Tell me about that." I felt him hesitate, but if they wanted me to trust them, I was going to need them to open up to me. I needed to feel like a part of them.

"I was dropped off on the doorstep of an orphanage when I was a baby." His fingers drifted mindlessly in circles up and down my back. "Once that place shut down, all us kids were put in different foster homes. I never had a kind one. As early as I can remember, I was always with someone who couldn't afford to feed us because all the money was going towards their drugs and/or alcohol. I had one foster parent who used to keep us locked in the basement all night and most of the day. Showers were a rarity, and our toilet was a single bucket that was kept in the corner."

I was appalled. The thought of Tristan as a little boy, kept in a basement, never knowing what love or family was like was enough to have my throat aching against the threat of tears. I knew I couldn't look at him or he would see the sadness written all over my face. He had compared our lives, but I grew up in a life of luxury. My parents may not have been the best. My dad may have eventually tried to kill me, but I was never locked in a basement, deprived of life, with a bucket in the corner.

"Anyway," he continued. "I was on the brink of just running away around the age of fourteen. Honestly, living on the street sounded better than living in any of the homes I was forced to live in as a kid." He sighed. "But then Elliot came into the picture. He became my friend, my brother. He gave me a place to go when life at my place was too much." He shrugged, and his hands moved to my hair.

"And we did what we had to do to survive. His parents were into some bad shit, and we kind of just followed their lead. We discovered we were good at it, really good at it. This whole thing just grew from there. Sebastian, the crazy fuck, came in later," he laughed to himself, and I found I really liked the sound.

"And you said the meeting tonight went too easily. So what do we do next? Where do we go from here?" I rolled onto my back, but his arms stayed around me. For cutthroat gangsters, they really liked to cuddle.

"I'd like to get you trained up. I want Elliot to get you to a point where we know you can handle your own shit. Not that we can't protect you, but we won't be around every minute of the day. I need Sebastian to get your marksmanship up to par. I don't expect you to be a sniper, but I also want you to be able to shoot and hit a moving target where they need to be hit."

"I'm excellent with a gun, thank you."

"You are. But you could be better."

I punched his bicep half-heartedly, and he just laughed. "Do you have anything good to say?"

"Hmm," he debated. "You're pretty good with your mouth."

I punched him again. Harder, this time. "Fuck off. When do I get to do some real stuff? Get out of this house with you guys on some real business?"

"Soon."

"Noncommittal."

"Get stronger. Get better. Earn our trust. I've got

some people that will have eyes on your father, watching and waiting to see what his next move might be. I don't trust him as far as I can throw him. And I couldn't throw that fat fuck very far." I rolled over again and pressed my back flush against his front and took some comfort in the solid build of his body.

"I just want to belong somewhere," I admitted. "I want a family."

"I know, Scarlet. I know," he whispered into my ear. "Get some sleep. We can talk more about this stuff later. We have nothing but time."

"You say that," I said through a yawn. "But he could come for me at any time. Don't let your guard down. He's smarter than he looks. And he knows where I am now."

"He might know we have you, but he doesn't know where you are."

I shrugged. He kissed the back of my head, and I eventually drifted off to the sound of his even breathing and the circles he drew lightly up and down my arm.

CHAPTER
sixteen

SCARLET

The next morning, I was training with Elliot when Sebastian found us. Elliot had me pinned, my face pressed hard into the mat, but when Sebastian came into the room, Elliot lost focus and I was able to swing my leg around and flip us over, pressing the imaginary knife against his throat. Sweat dripped off my face and onto his. He grimaced and let me win that round.

"Pinned ya, bitch."

He rolled his eyes and pushed me off of him. I landed hard on my ass with an oomph.

"We got word that Derek and his crew will be downtown tonight. We're going," Seb said.

Elliot nodded and started pulling the tape off of his hands.

"Who's Derek?" I asked.

"Head of a rival gang that's been trying to get in on our drug trade. But they cut their shit with Fentanyl to make more, make it seem cheaper," Sebastian explained. "And we don't like that."

"So, what's the plan?" Elliot scoffed at me. "What?" I asked. Sometimes the way he looked at me made me want to punch him right in his pretty mouth, knock some of those teeth out, and bring his looks down to a human standard.

"We aren't telling you shit," he said as he lifted his shirt to wipe sweat from his face, and I nearly face-planted the mat just trying to get a good look at them. "You'll stay home like a good little girl and be babysat."

"Actually, El…" Sebastian trailed off.

"Oh, you have got to be kidding me," Elliot said at the same time I yelled, "I get to come?"

"She gets to come," Sebastian said through a smile. He looked at me like it was Christmas morning. "Ready to come play with me, pet? Get some last-minute practice in before your debut? Maybe you can spill some blood again tonight."

"Uh, yes!" I said. "Let me just go get changed. I smell like sweat."

"I happen to like your sweat," he said, grabbing my bicep as I walked past him. He leaned his nose down to my neck and licked my shoulder to my ear, sending heat through my entire body.

"How did you convince Tristan to let her come?" Elliot asked, breaking our little bubble.

"I didn't," he said, letting my arm go put pulling me under his. "It was Tristan's idea, so if you have an issue with it, you can bring it up with him." He turned me and led me out the door. "We leave at six!" he threw over his shoulder.

The entire drive into the city was filled with loud, angry music and absolutely zero conversation. I had run to the car, pushing Elliot's big ass out of the way to get to the front seat thinking I would be able to have some sort of control over the radio, but Tristan gave me a firm look and shook his head. I hadn't seen a lot of his scary looks since that first night, but that was definitely one I was going to obey. I wondered what that look would do to me in bed and mentally filed that thought away for another time.

We pulled up to an abandoned warehouse with Corpse blasting from the speakers, his deep voice filling my body with a nervous energy. I finally started to feel butterflies in my stomach. I couldn't believe they had actually let me come. The guns resting against my sides felt heavier as we pulled into a darkened corner that looked like it used to be used as a loading dock. Tristan had strapped me with two guns—that was all I was permitted for this little outing. But he had also given me a couple of knives that I had strapped to my ankles, concealed by the boots I was wearing. Tristan turned the music down.

"*This* is where we're going? When you said downtown, I thought it would be like a bar or a restaurant or something." I felt three sets of eyes burn into my face, but I just ignored them and continued to look up at the warehouse. Elliot laughed and mumbled something under his breath that didn't feel like a compliment.

"You thought there would be a drug trade operation happening out of a bar? Where are they going to make drugs in a bar?" Elliot asked.

"Whoa, whoa," I said, turning to face them. "I thought when we were discussing this that we were just going to intercept them selling the drugs and scare the shit out of them. We are literally walking into the heart of their fucking business?"

"Yeah, babe," Sebastian chimed in like an excited puppy. "Cut them off at the balls."

I blew out a breath. "Alright then," I said, yanking my hair up into a knot. "What's the plan?"

"The plan is," Tristan said, watching me with weary eyes. "The plan is you follow us in, but you stay back. I don't want them knowing we have you with us. I don't want you seen."

"Then why the fuck am I even here? I thought I was here to help."

"And how are you going to help, princess?" Elliot asked. On Seb's mouth, princess sounded hot. On Elliot's mouth, it sounded like an insult. I rolled my eyes.

"You guys seem to think I am some sort of pillow princess that has never lifted a finger in her life. I will have you know that growing up in a life like this makes you hard. Just because I came from wealth doesn't mean that I was born with a silver spoon up my ass. I was expected to learn how to run a business, fight, and shoot to kill. So excuse the fuck out of me if I assumed I would be put to some use instead of having to hang back and watch like some sort of fifties housewife."

I took a breath and looked at all of them. Sebastian and Tristan looked like scolded puppies, but Elliot just sat there, his arms crossed and a fucking smirk on his face that made me want to slap it off.

"The decision has been made. Hang back. Be a shadow. Let's go." Elliot opened his door and climbed out. The other guys followed suit, and I crawled out of mine with a huff, still pissed I wasn't going to see any action. I felt ready. Sure, I hadn't been training with Elliot for months, but I was a quick student, and I knew I could handle myself. And Seb had really sharpened my shooting skills. I knew I could fucking help, and I was just going to have to prove it to them.

Seb twisted a silencer onto the end of one of his many guns he had strapped to his body. I had watched him put each one on earlier, and it had gotten me so hot I had left the room to take a cold shower before getting dressed myself. I had stopped questioning the shit that made me horny lately. Clearly I was fucked in the head, but so were they, so whatever. I liked what I liked.

He pointed the gun at the thick chain keeping one of the side doors locked and shot. First try, that thing fell into a heap on the ground. When I looked at him, he just winked and pushed me behind him as they all filtered inside in front of me. It took a minute for my eyes to adjust in the darkness. It was dark outside, and there were zero lights on, so I just grabbed the back of

Seb's shirt and followed them down the empty hallways.

"Intel says they're in the down downstairs," Tristan whispered down our line of bodies. "When we get down there, Scar, I want you to stay hidden, but keep an eye out for anyone not in the main room. Give us a whistle if you see someone coming. Do not, I repeat, do *not* engage. Do you understand?"

I stared at him through the darkness. Had I heard him correctly?

"Did you just say 'the down downstairs'?" I asked.

Seb laughed. "It's what he calls the basement." I held back my own laughter and heard an exasperated sigh come from the front of the line.

"Can you please just agree on our terms? Stay hidden, stay safe?" Tristan almost sounded embarrassed.

"Yes, sir," I said in a sweet voice. Both Sebastian and Tristan groaned. Seb grabbed his crotch and looked back at me.

"Don't say stuff like that right now, princess. I'm trying to focus, and I can't focus if I want to tear those tight leather pants off of you and fuck you against the wall." I pressed my thighs together at the thought but just nodded. The look in his eyes was all too serious.

"Can we please just go and get this over with? You both can get your dicks wet when we get home," Grumpy sighed.

"At the same time? Yes, please." Two more groans from Tristan and Seb.

"Is that a promise?" Seb asked. I laughed and

pushed him to keep following the others. But yes, it was most definitely a promise. Maybe that could be their reward if I got out of there alive.

We descended down into the basement, each step more precarious than the last with the light dwindling. When we rounded the corner, a soft yellow light started to permeate the darkness. I watched the guys' backs, tense from holding their guns at their chests, and followed, trying to keep myself against the walls to blend in with the shadows. When we crept out of the stairwell, there was music pouring out from some double doors down the hall.

"Well, at least we know they won't hear you coming," I muttered into Seb's back. "Is that…Nickelback?" I made a gagging noise, and I felt Seb chuckle through my grip on his shirt. I hadn't realized I was still holding on to him. I unclenched my fingers and let my hands fall idly to my sides.

"Yep, that would be Nickelback," he confirmed.

"Gross."

We moved up to the doors, and I crossed behind them, moving to the corner where I could be almost invisible unless someone was looking for me. From that spot, I would be able to see someone coming for those doors at any angle. Tristan looked at me and nodded.

"Stay hidden. Stay safe."

"Yes, yes, I've got it. Stay out of the way." He walked over and took my face in his hands. The look on his face took my breath away. And then when he kissed me, I realized why he was being so annoying. He was worried. He broke the kiss and looked at me. "Stop worrying about me. You need to focus to keep yourself safe," I whispered so only he could hear. He nodded and walked back to the guys.

"Alright, when we burst through those doors, keep your eyes open and your guns ready." Sebastian and Elliot both nodded. Tristan blew out a breath and then turned towards the double doors with the other two at his back.

He kicked open the doors and strutted in like he owned the place. Sebastian looked over at me briefly and winked before setting off inside after them. The second those doors were open, a soft floral but also very chemical smell came wafting out, and I nearly gagged on the sickly sweet scent. I couldn't hear much over the music blasting through the room, and once the doors swung closed again, I was completely shut off from whatever conversations were happening.

I took deep breaths, trying to slow my heartbeat so that I could hear any noises that weren't coming from inside. I was shifting from one foot to the other, nervous energy racking through my body. There had to be more people in this place. It was huge, and there was no way the bosses would be in that room. But there was also no way they would leave it unprotected.

Not thirty seconds later, I heard footfalls on the stairwell. *Fuck.* I grabbed both guns out of the holsters and aimed them at the door we had just come out of only a few minutes ago. Fuck whistling, I was not about to let a hoard of men bust through those doors and possibly kill one of them.

"Oh, shit," I whispered to myself as the doors burst

open. Person after person ran through those doors. There had to be at least ten of them running down the hall and straight towards the crack den. I didn't even think—I just started shooting. I aimed for chests and foreheads, watching each guy drop to the ground like a sack of fucking potatoes. I was shooting so quickly they barely had time to get any shots off in my direction. But I was hidden, so they couldn't even aim. Maybe Tristan had a point after all.

I laughed as the last one looked towards the corner where I was, practically shitting himself as he realized all of his guys were now dead on the floor. I took aim one last time and popped a bullet right in between his eyes. I blew on the barrel like I was straight out of an old Western and smiled. *That was fun.*

And then shots started popping off behind those doors. The doors my boys had gone through. *My* boys. I smiled and walked over to one of the men on the floor and ran my fingers through the warm puddle of blood. I streaked it across my cheeks like war paint, grabbed two more guns, and then kicked open the doors.

CHAPTER
seventeen

ELLIOT

"Honey, I'm home!" she screamed as she burst through the damn doors like fucking Rambo. The music drowned out most of her words, but we all got the gist. This bitch was fucking insane and most definitely had a death wish storming into a crack den blind like that. I could feel all of us go still in the middle of the fight to look at her.

Is that…is that blood on her face?

The guy I had just knocked to the ground swung out his leg, and I hit the floor hard. *Fuck's sake*, I thought. She was too much of a distraction to have around. Once I had hit the ground, he took a moment to rove his eyes over her body.

I shot him in his eye.

CHAPTER
eighteen

TRISTAN

She had smeared blood all over her beautiful fucking face like war paint. It really made those blue eyes pop. She had a wide smile across her face, and she was holding two semi-automatic rifles that were definitely not ours, cocked against her hips. Had she already used all the ammo in the guns I had given her? Twenty fucking rounds? How many men had she just killed outside those doors in the five minutes we had left her alone? My dick twitched at the mental image that rendered.

The guy I had been grappling with got in a good punch, and the pain that shot across my jaw was enough to bring me back to the present. A lot of the workers had run off when we burst in, but the higher-ups that happened to be in here stayed around to try and protect their shit. We had gotten a few shots in before it turned into an outright brawl. Those baby blues of hers found me, and she smiled.

CHAPTER
nineteen

SEBASTIAN

My own personal demon walked through those doors, guns fucking blazing, covered in blood, and dripping in sex. I could have thrown her down on top of the dead bodies and blood at my feet and fucked her right there. Fuck me, she looked beautiful. She pushed some stray hair out of her face with one of the guns and winked at Tristan before finding me. Her eyes drifted down my body until they found my rock-hard cock. She licked her lips and then met my eyes again.

Oh yeah. I was definitely going to fill that mouth later.

CHAPTER twenty

SCARLET

The "honey, I'm home" bit did not perform as well as I had hoped. I was hoping for at least a few laughs, but all three of them just stared at me like I had lost my mind. Maybe it was the blood smeared all over my face, but still, they could've at least given me a smile. Selfish fucks.

They did all stop in the middle of their individual fights to look at me, and my ego soaked it up like a sponge. I expected it to be chaos when I walked in. But as I looked around, they had pretty much been able to either subdue or kill anyone that was still left in the open room. The smell was terrible though. My nose burned with the scent.

Elliot was grappling on the ground with a guy and finally got sick of it and pressed the barrel of his gun to the dude's forehead and shot. Blood spattered onto his face, and he sagged over onto the ground, panting and gripping his side. His hand turned red with blood, and I ran over to him, kneeling next to his side.

"Did you get yourself fucking stabbed?" I asked him as I pulled his hand away from his side. He winced but let me roll up his shirt to look. The gash was torn and bleeding with every ragged breath he took.

"I'm fine. Let's just torch this fucking place and go," he ground out. I rolled my eyes and took off the gun holsters and then slipped my shirt over my head. His eyes drifted to my sports bra where I could feel my nipples straining against the chill. He groaned and laid his head back. I just smiled.

"Shut up. You aren't going anywhere until this is wrapped around to try and help stop the bleeding." I rolled up the torso of the shirt and placed it against the wound. I had been wearing long sleeves, so I stretched them across his hard stomach and then under his back and tied them together on the opposite side. I really had to stretch and pull them for it to work, but at least it was pressing tightly against the wound.

Just as I finished, "Crazy Bitch" by Buckcherry started blasting out of the speakers, and a new group of guys kicked down the doors I had just come from.

"Well," I said, picking my guns back up and crawling over Elliot to block his body from further assault, "at least they have some good taste in music." Before they could see me move, I aimed and shot four of them. Their bodies crumpled to the ground, but when I tried to shoot the two others that had burst in,

Elliot grabbed me around the waist, flipping me over his body until he was on top of me. The shots I had gotten off before he rolled me over pinged off the ceiling.

"What the fuck, Elliot?" His hair fell limp around his face, and his eyes were so dark they almost looked black as they looked down at me. His entire body was flush against mine with his forearms on either side of my face to hold himself up. He winced at the pain in his side. I tried to shimmy out from under him, but it was like lying under a house. More shots rang out from the other side of the room.

"Stop. Moving." His voice came out deep and rough. I felt him grow hard against my belly, and I smirked up at him.

"Happy to see me, babe?" I reached up and gave him a peck on the nose. "Now get off of me," I said before I pressed my fingers into his wound. He let out a not-so-manly scream before falling off me. I knew it was a low blow, but he wasn't going to keep me from helping the other guys. I sat up and grabbed one of the tables that were nearby. I pushed it over, drug supplies scattering across the floor, and yanked it in front of both of us. I peeked over the top, and a bullet flew past my head.

"Holy shit," I muttered, dropping back below the table. "I almost got shot in the face!" I exclaimed to Elliot and laughed. He just groaned and looked at me with a death stare. I was probably going to pay for that little move later.

Worth it.

I felt a little manic with all the adrenaline pumping through my veins. I tried to steady my breathing as I heard more gunfire. I looked over at where I had last seen Tristan and Seb. The former was gripping what looked like a graze wound on his arm while the latter had been able to take the rest of them out. Seb crouched down to look at Tristan's wound and gave me a nice view of his ass which I appreciated.

Pulling my eyes from his shapely bum, I looked around the room, taking count of how many people we had killed in the span of fifteen minutes. It was a lot. I was actually impressed. I scrunched my nose at the dried blood on my face. It was really starting to itch now that it was getting crusty. Probably should've thought of that before I decided to smear it all over my cheeks. I had made it to the count of ten dead bodies when I saw someone reaching for a gun, his fingers straining at the effort.

I stood up from behind the table and watched him struggle. He was so focused on getting the gun and not being seen by Sebastian and Tristan that he didn't even see me make my way over to him. I had only made it a few steps before his fingers finally gripped the gun, and he slowly lifted it. It was pointed directly at Seb.

I saw red. Every rational thought flew out of my head. I could hear my blood roaring in my ears.

"Hey," I said loud enough for him to hear over the music that was still blaring. Was anyone going to turn that off? He turned his head towards me, and the gun quickly followed. There was the vague feeling of being pushed in the shoulder, hard. I realized he had shot me.

The fucker had *shot* me. Once I had recognized what happened, pain shot through my shoulder like a white-hot poker.

"Motherfucker," I said under my breath. I saw his finger squeeze the trigger a few more times in a panic as I made my way over to him, but nothing came out. I felt the sadistic smile creep over my face. I must've really looked the part because this asshole pissed his pants when I finally reached him and kicked the gun out of his hand. He screamed in pain, and my smile only grew wider. I straddled his waist, well above the puddle of piss in his pants, and grabbed one of the knives out of my boot.

"You tried to kill my boys," I said sweetly as I flicked open the blade and admired it. He held up his hands and babbled something about being sorry. "Too late, babes," I said before stabbing the knife into the side of his throat. I wasn't sure exactly where the carotid artery was, but I was pretty sure I hit it with the amount of blood gushing out of the wound and onto my hand.

I pulled the knife out of his neck as gurgled noises came out of his mouth. I reared back and stabbed him again. And again. One for each of my boys. Then again for the asshole that tried to rape me. Again for the father that tried to have me killed. And again. And again. And again. I lost track of how many times I actually stabbed him.

All I could feel was the flesh and muscle tearing. His body twitched between my legs with each puncture. My vision blurred, and my throat was so dry it ached. I realized I was crying. And screaming. I was raising my good arm above my head, gripping the knife so tightly that my fingers went white underneath all of the blood, and then throwing my weight behind each thrust into his body. I was a woman possessed. I shoved it into his chest one last time with one final scream. My body shook with sobs.

"Scarlet."

"What!" I whipped my head around, my hand still bloody and clinging to the knife embedded deep in dude's chest, the other arm hanging limply at my side. Seb was crouched behind me, his eyes soft but other parts of him very, very hard. I licked my lips, and the iron taste of blood coated my tongue.

"He's dead, pet." He reached out and grabbed my bad arm, pulling me onto his lap. I screamed at the pain, but it only seemed to spur him on. His eyes were like a wild animal, almost predatory. He ran his hands over my face and then down to my neck. I could feel the fresh blood smear across my skin. His eyes heated as they found the bullet wound. He gave it a rough squeeze, and I whimpered as more tears fell down my cheeks, but my pussy throbbed at the pain. He smiled like he knew what he was doing to me. Like he knew how fucked-up I was that the pain of getting shot and the act of killing someone had gotten me wet.

My hands reached up and gripped his face, smashing it to my own. He parted his mouth instantly. It wasn't a kiss; it was a fight. Our tongues wrestled as our teeth clashed. I tasted my tears, blood from either the roughness of our kiss or the dead body next to us, it didn't matter, and something that was just utterly Seb. I loved the taste of him, and I rolled my hips against him just to show him how much.

A hand fisted in the knot of hair on top of my head and yanked backwards, breaking the kiss. Sebastian paid no mind and just continued kissing, licking, and sucking his way down my neck. My heartbeat had dropped straight to my cunt. I could feel it pulsating against his zipper.

I looked up into Tristan's heated gaze. He watched Seb move along my neck and collarbone and then back up to my jaw. His grip in my hair tightened, and I moaned at the pain in my scalp. His eyes dropped to my chest where I knew the sports bra was doing wonders for my cleavage. I pushed my chest out, wanting him to look, to want. His nostrils flared, and he took a deep breath, trying to gather himself. Seb's rough hand had pushed up under my bra and was rolling a nipple between his fingers.

My orgasm started building already. I could feel my face flush, the heat build in my core, and shivers spider-webbing across my skin. I was panting when his fingers found the other nipple. Tristan twisted his fingers tighter in my hair and then leaned over, claiming my mouth with his own. I ground against Sebastian faster and harder, my pussy begging for release. I felt the flush crawl up my neck and across my face.

When Tristan broke the kiss, my eyes found Elliot. He was standing across the room, watching the three of us and idly rubbing the bulge of his pants. Tristan's hand wrapped around my throat and squeezed, blocking off my air supply. My gaze drifted back to him as I opened my mouth and stuck out my tongue.

"Good girl," he cooed and spat in my mouth. Sebastian twisted my nipple painfully as he bit into my shoulder. My eyes found Elliot's again as I swallowed against Tristan's grip.

"Come," Elliot commanded. And with one more roll against Sebastian's hard cock beneath me, I did. Fireworks shot through my body all the way down to my toes, and I damn near screamed from how hard it hit me. Tristan's grip relaxed, and my head fell against Seb's shoulder as I tried to breathe and came down from the orgasm.

"Nice distraction trick," I said against his shoulder. He laughed.

"Something had to bring you back from wherever you had gone," he said.

"We need to get a doctor to look at your bullet wound and Elliot's stab wound," Tristan said.

I peeled myself off Sebastian and stood on weak legs. I followed them all out of the room, up the stairs, and out of the warehouse, all of us sweaty and covered in blood. I probably should've been more shocked that I had just gotten off after killing more than a dozen people, but I was too exhausted and in too much pain to care. And I wasn't going to be ashamed of what got me off anymore.

"You get her settled in the car. Seb and I will take care of this place," Tristan said to Elliot.

"Fire time!" Sebastian squealed excitedly. They got some stuff out of the back of the car as Elliot opened the back door and gestured for me to crawl in. The other two jogged back into the building.

"Lie down," Elliot ordered. As gingerly as I could without putting weight on my bad arm, I twisted and slowly lay down across the seats. He shut the door and walked around to the other side. When he opened the door, his upper body was bare save for my shirt wrapped around his belly. "Here," he said, lifting my head and laying it on his thigh after he climbed in.

He wrapped his shirt around my shoulder and applied so much pressure my head swam with the pain. I let out a loud groan. I was going to pass out. My vision was going black, and my face and chest went cold and hot at the same time.

"Elliot…I'm gonna…"

CHAPTER
twenty one

SCARLET

For an entire week, none of the guys would let me leave my bed. It was fucking excruciating to just lie there and watch TV and heal. I did manage to get through a lot of seasons of *Grey's Anatomy* though.

The doctor they kept on their payroll was hovering over my shoulder, prodding here and there and making me slowly lift my arm up and down. It was still stiff as hell, but I had been doing my exercises every day, and it seemed to be getting better. I gritted my teeth through the pain and gave him a wide, fake smile when he looked down at me.

"I think you're okay to start moving around again. But maybe we take it easy and try not to get shot?" Humor lit up his eyes, and I gave him a pity laugh.

"What about training?" Seb asked from across the

room where he had been watching. He had been watching very closely every time the doctor came by just to make sure his hands weren't going anywhere they didn't need to be going. For someone who had already shared me with Tristan and seemed to be okay with it if Elliot wanted to join in as well, he was extremely possessive.

"She needs to get full range of motion back from this arm before she starts back into anything too heavy. Just nothing that puts too much strain on that left shoulder."

"Thanks, Doc."

The doctor nodded and gathered his things. "I'll go see Mr. Elliot now and then be on my way. Let me know if you need anything at all. Okay, miss?"

I smiled and waited until he was out of the room before I stood out of the covers and made my way over to the bathroom. Sebastian followed behind me. He had taken over the role of my caregiver, and bath time seemed to be his favorite time.

"Care to let me fuck that pretty little pussy of yours, pet?" I turned the water on and then spun around and threw my shirt over my head with my good arm, leaving me in nothing but my panties. I laughed while I watched him undress as quickly as humanly possible. His erection stood proudly out from his body, a drop of precum already glistening above his piercing. He advanced on me, slipping his thumbs into the sides of my thong and pulling to down to the floor for me to step out of.

He walked us into the shower and pressed my back

up against the cold tile. I let out a little yelp, but with the head of his cock pressing against my entrance, it quickly turned into a moan. Seb gripped my jaw, and I locked eyes with him for as long as I could as he slowly slid inside of me. At some point, my eyes rolled into the back of my head at the pure bliss of him filling me up, that piercing dragging along all the right nerves.

"I love the way you feel around my cock. You're so fucking tight," he groaned against my neck. "We've got a meeting downstairs with the guys, so this is going to have to be quick, I'm afraid."

"Oh, just shut up and fuck me, Seb." I gripped his hair as he let out one last groan before slipping completely out of me and then slamming back in. I gripped his shoulders with my good arm and his hair with my other while he fucked me into oblivion.

"Do you like that, precious?" His breath was hot on my ear, and his words sent shivers down my spine. "Are you my dirty little slut?" I let out a whimper as he slammed inside of me. God I fucking loved it when he talked to me like that. Never in a million years would I have ever let a guy talk to me like that outside of the bedroom, but at times like this, it went straight to my pussy. "Answer me." A wave of fire spread through my body

"Yes, sir," I said into his hair that I still had in a vise grip. "I'm your dirty little slut." I knew exactly what he wanted to hear. "Fuck me harder, please, Seb. I'm so close." I was a simpering mess around his cock as his thumb gently rolled around my clit. He lifted his head and watched me as he squeezed my clit, and I fell over the edge, sparks igniting at the base of my spine and spreading out into my fingers and toes.

"Fuck," he whimpered. I loved it when he was so lost in me that he couldn't even be bothered to act tough anymore. Like he couldn't actually get enough of me. He may have been a tough-as-shit gangbanger, but I was able to bring him to his knees. With one more hard thrust that damn near pushed me through the wall, he came inside of me, his breath panting against my neck.

I kissed his hair, and he let me slide down his body, his cock sliding out of me easily with both of our releases coating it. His arms caged me in against the wall, and I smiled up at him. I trailed my fingers up over his chiseled abs and across his pecs, following the outlines of his tattoos. He blew out a breath and looked at me with his pretty brown eyes. I was still caught off guard by how handsome he was.

"So I've been meaning to ask..." I let my voice trail off. I had been meaning to talk to him about the whole sharing me thing with him for a while now, but it had never felt like the right time. I could also probably chalk it up to me being a pussy when it came to communicating my feelings. I inwardly cringed at the thought.

"Yes, pet?" He leaned down and kissed my cheek, nuzzling into my hair.

"Do you really not care about sharing me with Tristan?" His mouth caught my ear and then moved down my neck, making my breath catch in my throat.

"Who am I to make you choose?" He licked up the side of my neck. "I'm happy to share you if that's what makes you happy. Don't overthink it. Tristan and I don't give a fuck about it." I sighed a happy sigh, content to let that be the truth for the time being. I was still going to have to talk to Tristan about it, and if I was ever able to break down Elliot's walls, he was going to have to get on board with this as well. My boys. My little harem. I smiled up at him.

"Want to help me clean up so that we can go to this little meeting you were talking about?" I kissed his chest, trailing my tongue over his skin. He gave a small shudder and then grabbed my face into a punishing kiss. His tongue darted into my mouth, claiming it as his, sweeping it across my own. He spun us around and backed me into the warm spray of the water, soaking my hair before letting go of my mouth with a growl.

"Let's get you cleaned up, sweet cheeks." He smacked my ass and then proceeded to wash my hair.

———

The other two were already sitting in the living room when Seb and I made our way downstairs. I had stolen a pair of his sweatpants and one of his shirts to wear. Everything smelled like him, and I pulled the shirt up over my nose as I curled up next to Tristan. He pulled me onto his lap and began plaiting my hair.

I watched Elliot from across the room. I hadn't seen him since that night since we were both banished to our respective rooms to heal. His torso was bare as well, and he had a clean patch on his side where he had been stabbed. Other than that, he looked perfect. My finger itched to go play with his hair that he had decided to wear down. It grazed his broad shoulders, and when I looked up at his face, he was staring back at me. I winked and earned myself an eye roll.

Progress.

I leaned back into Tristan's chest as he finished with my hair and let him wrap his arms around my waist.

"I got the all clear today," I said, pulling Seb's shirt off my face.

"She got the half clear," Seb corrected. I flipped him off and settled further into Tristan's lap. Tristan laughed and gave me a squeeze.

"Alright, then, now that my medical updates are out, how's Elliot's stab wound?"

"It's fine," he grunted. I rolled my eyes.

"Okay," I drawled. "Why're we having a little family meeting?"

"We got some new intel about Derek and the MadDawgs."

"Wait," I interrupted. "That's the name of their fucking gang?" I asked, laughing. Tristan nodded. "The MadDawgs? Jesus Christ, what a name."

"I agree, precious. And not only is their name idiotic, they're proving themselves to be just as stupid. Our new intel tells us they've decided to put their hat in with your family, Scar. We think that's why they started trying to push their agenda in our area. Your family is trying to get a foothold in our city in total disregard for our truce."

"Well, I feel like we kind of saw this coming," I said.

"We did. But that doesn't mean I'm any less annoyed that I have to deal with it now. They know it was us that went in guns blazing, killing a lot of their crew, and then burned down their primary drug factory. To say the least, they're pissed," Tristan said on a laugh. It rumbled through my body.

"What's our next move?" Elliot asked from across the room.

"Keep our eyes and ears open. Make sure we stay a step ahead of any plans they may have for us. They've gone silent for now, no doubt probably trying to rebuild after we took out such an important aspect of their operation." Seb and Elliot both nodded. "And I'd also like to get Scarlet here a job. She needs something to do, and if she is going to be a part of this fucked-up family, she's going to need to pull her weight."

"What did you have in mind?" Sebastian asked as Elliot simultaneously groaned. I smiled at how annoyed he was going to be that the other two were really starting to trust me.

"I'm going to take her into the city today and show her around the Tower."

"The Tower? What the fuck is that?" I asked.

"The Tower is what we call our main building of business. We call it the Tower because it quite literally looks like a tower. It's one of the tallest buildings in the city."

"And what are your plans for me there?"

"I'm going to introduce you to some people and then let you get to know our cybersecurity team. And while you do that, I'll get some much-needed work done that I've been putting off in the time you've been here. I've also got some meetings dotted throughout the afternoon." Butterflies swam in my stomach. I was ecstatic I was finally being trusted with something that I would actually be good at. I could finally be useful.

"About time you guys see my worth," I said, sticking my nose in the air.

"That has yet to be proven," Elliot mumbled.

"When do we leave?"

"In an hour. So go get dressed and have some lunch, and then we will head into the city."

"Do I even have clothes in there as nice as yours for like, a work environment like that?" I chewed on my nails, a nervous habit that sometimes came back when I was worried about something new. Tristan gently grabbed my hand and pulled it down away from my mouth.

"We've made sure that you've got any possible outfit combination you could ever want or need. But this isn't some stuck-up corporate office, babe. And even if it was, you're one of us now, and that means if you wanted to walk in there naked, you could."

I snorted.

"Warn me first if you're going to go in there naked, though, please. Because one of us will need to go in there first and warn anyone that if they look at you, I'll start breaking extremities," Sebastian said. "On second thought, Tristan. I'd prefer no one look at her anyway," he said darkly.

"How am I supposed to get any work done if no one can even look at me?" He huffed, pouting. I stood up off Tristan's lap and made my way over to Seb. I kissed him and whispered in his ear. "And if anyone looks at me, you can punish me for it later." I bit his ear, and he groaned. I laughed and ran up the stairs to get ready before he could grab me.

"That better be a fucking promise!" he shouted up the stairs after me.

CHAPTER
twenty two

TRISTAN

Scarlet looked at me and back to the bike and then back to me, her eyes wide and excited.

"We get to take that?" She was practically squealing. I figured the poor girl needed some excitement after she had been stuck in her bed for the past week. So I decided to bring out the Ducati and let her have some fun.

"We do," I said and handed her a helmet. She looked sexy as hell holding that helmet under her arm, walking around the bike with stars in her eyes. She was dressed in heeled biker boots, ripped black jeans, and some sort of loose top that showed off all her beautiful tattoos when she didn't have her leather jacket on.

"She's beautiful," she murmured as she ran her hands along the bike.

"Ready to go?"

"Yes!"

"Have you ridden on a bike like this before?" She rolled her eyes at my question and strapped the helmet on. "I'm just making sure you know how to ride bitch." I smirked at her. She reared back and punched me hard on the arm.

"Shut up and get on the bike, Tristan," she said and flicked her visor down. I put on my own helmet and swung my leg over, leaning forward so that she could climb on as well. Her small frame fit perfectly on the bike, and she hugged my body like a koala. I turned the key and revved the engine, feeling the bike purr beneath us. Scar's thighs clenched tighter around me, and I smiled to myself.

Yeah, this is going to be a fun ride.

We took off towards the city, and I felt her grip my waist just a little harder until she got used to the feeling again. During a straight stretch, she leaned away from my body and threw her hands out to the sides and dropped her head back. I couldn't hear her laughing, but I could feel it tumble through her as she brought herself back and held on tight again. I wished I could see what she looked like under the visor, smile stretched wide, her face pink with excitement.

It was a relatively long drive into the city, but I loved every moment of it. I took her on as many quiet roads as I could so that we could go as fast as I wanted. Not that I was worried about getting a ticket—we had the police in our pockets, but the stop would've been annoying.

When we pulled up to the Tower, I circled into the underground parking deck and into my private, locked area. She climbed off the bike and yanked off the helmet. Her hair had fallen out of the plait and stood up at all angles. Pure joy was written all over her face from her smile to her bright eyes. She was so beautiful. And all three of us were in such deep shit. I took off my own helmet and hung it from the handlebars before grabbing her waist and pulling her over to me. I needed to taste her, to taste that happiness.

She threw her good arm around my shoulders and kissed me. God, she smelled good. She always smelled like some sort of flower, but underneath that, there was that hint of petrol. It was just so Scarlet that it made my chest hurt. Her tongue brushed across mine, and I pulled her a bit tighter against me before she ended the kiss and pushed away.

"Let's get to work, boss man." She hung her helmet from the other handlebar, and we locked the garage as we left and entered the lift. "How many floors are there?"

"Seventy-three."

"And what floor will I be on?"

"Seventy-three," I answered again.

"The cybersecurity people are important enough to be on the top floor?" Her nose scrunched up. I reached out and booped it. Quick as lightning, she reached out and twisted my finger just enough for it to hurt.

"Don't boop my nose, jackass."

"But it's so cute." I gave her a wink before pulling out of her grip and twisting her arm behind her back to push her up against the wall of the lift. She grunted and yanked against my hold, but I was too strong for her, especially with her weakened shoulder. "Ready to apologize for that little outburst?"

"Fuck you." I smiled and pressed my crotch against her ass where she would be able to feel just how much I was willing to fuck her. My cock twitched at the thought of taking her from behind right there in the lift. She pressed her ass back against me just enough to tell me she wanted it too.

"Another time, love," I whispered into her ear. I smacked her ass with my other hand and then let her go.

"You never answered my question," she said, rolling her eyes as she watched me adjust myself. I needed to get myself under control before the doors opened up and everyone saw my raging hard-on.

"No. The cybersecurity people are not on the top floor. But I am. So that's where I expect you to be."

"How am I supposed to work with them if I'm not even on the same floor?" Her nose scrunched up again, and I fought hard to not reach out and touch it again.

"Scarlet, they're not going to be working with you. They're going to be working for you." Her eyes went wide for a moment before that news settled in. None of us ever expected her to just be another employee. Well, maybe Elliot did. But at some point he had to realize she was way more important to us, to all of us. We were giving her the entire department to run.

"You're letting me run your entire cybersecurity department?"

"We are. So let's hope you're as good as you say you are. Time to prove yourself, love."

The lift dinged and opened out onto the top floor of the building. We stepped out, and I guided her over to my office that had floor-to-ceiling windows with an amazing view of the city. I took off my jacket and threw it over the back of one of the sofas before making my way over to my desk. I sifted through the directory and dialed out to my top admin and watched as she gazed out across the city.

"Mr. Grange?" Melody's voice sounded through the speaker.

"Melody, I've brought the new head of the cybersecurity department in with me today. Could you please come get Scarlet and show her around, introduce her, et cetera? I have some meetings to attend to this afternoon." Scarlet looked back at me over her shoulder and then started circling the room, taking it all in. I'll admit, the first time I saw my office, I was impressed too.

I hadn't spared a single expense making it look as rich as possible. It had the most expensive-looking furniture we could find, a large electric fireplace on the opposite wall from my desk, and lush carpet. I wanted every client that came into this office to know who they were dealing with.

"Of course, Mr. Grange. I will be right up."

"Is Melody pretty?" Scarlet asked from behind me, her voice a little more quiet than what I was used to.

"Why, love? Jealous?" I turned around to face her and leaned against my desk. She shrugged, her tough-girl armor fully back in place.

"I spoke to Sebastian earlier today about all of us," she said, still making her way around the office. "You guys all know I've been with both you and Seb in some sort of way." She paused and looked at me. Her awkwardness was written all over her face. Even the way she was standing was unusual for her. Scarlet was normally so sure of herself, but right now she looked vulnerable. All I wanted to do was pull her into my arms, but I knew she needed to get this out.

Sebastian had told me what she had told him earlier. She was worried that she would end up having to choose one of us. Seb and I had agreed a while back though that it wasn't right to make her do that. And, truthfully, neither of us minded sharing her. We shared everything else in life, and he was someone I trusted completely. Did I like to think of her on anyone's dick other than my own? No. But I wasn't going to make her make a decision she clearly didn't want to make. She could be *our* girl.

"So is that going to be a problem? Sharing me? And what if Elliot enters the equation as well? Are you guys going to be okay with me being with all of you?" She planted her hands on the back of the couch that was across from my desk. Her fingers gripped into the soft fabric, and I smiled at her, trying to put her at ease.

"Babe, you were ours the moment Sebastian tackled you in the woods. *All* of ours." I made my way over to her and took her face in my hands. "I want you to stop worrying about this. As long as I get a piece of you, I am more than happy to share you with them. But only us." I felt a mood come over me at the thought of her with anyone else but us. "If anyone else touches you, I will flay the skin from their body." She smiled. "Understood?"

"Understood." I slanted my mouth across hers, and she opened hers immediately. She tasted like cherries and something else that was just so *Scarlet* it made my head spin. A knock at the door had me reluctantly pulling away from her.

"Come in," I called to Melody. The sweet older woman with greying hair and an outfit any grandmother would be envious of walked in and smiled widely at Scarlet.

"Mr. Grange, how lovely to see you again. And you must be Scarlet!" She advanced on us and took Scarlet into her arms. Scar's eyes went wide as saucers, and I held back my laughter. Melody always had been a hugger. From the day she interviewed for us all those years ago, she had been the mother hen, always making sure we were eating and taking care of ourselves.

"Lovely to meet you," Scarlet wheezed.

Melody let her go and patted her cheeks before turning to me. "Are you all taking care of yourselves? I haven't seen you in far too long. You look too skinny." She poked my stomach, and I slung my arm around her shoulders and pulled her in for a hug.

"Melody, we are fine. But you're right, we haven't been around enough lately. How about we all have dinner tonight at the loft?" Her eyes lit up.

"I would love that."

"Now, Scar," I said, turning my attention back on her. "Don't let Melody here fool you. She's all smiles and hugs now, but this woman is tough as nails. She doesn't take any shit from anyone."

"Exactly," Melody said as she looped her arm through Scarlet's. "So if any of those boys give you any issues, you come to me and I'll handle it." Scarlet looked at me and smirked.

Great.

"Same goes for anyone here. Anything you need, anyone bothering you, you let me know. I will take care of it."

"Perfect, thank you," Scarlet said.

"I'll have her back in a few hours when your meetings are done," Melody said. And with one last smile, Scarlet followed her out of my office and to the fiftieth floor where she would get acquainted with everyone. I sighed and ran my hands through my hair, looking out the windows over the city.

I didn't know what the fuck we were going to do about her family. If they were still trying to test us, to take over our shit, we were going to have a problem. I knew that meeting with them had gone too smoothly. The pit in my stomach grew. What if taking and keeping his kid had the opposite effect? What if we had just pissed him off instead of tightening the leash?

"Fuck." I picked up my jacket and hung it up before making my way back behind my desk. Just a few meetings to get me through the afternoon and then a dinner. Then I would worry about what our next step was going to be in this mess we created.

I sent off a quick text to the boys to let them know we were going to have dinner with Melody at the loft tonight and then settled in to get ready for the meetings I had slotted for the next few hours. I hoped Scarlet enjoyed her afternoon much more than I was about to enjoy mine. As much as it frightened me, I wanted her to want to stick around.

CHAPTER
twenty three

SCARLET

After three whole hours of touring the Tower and meeting far too many people, Melody dropped me off at the lift. I pulled my hair out of its plait and massaged my scalp. In the span of a couple of weeks, my life had completely changed, and it was causing a whirlwind of emotions.

I chewed on my tongue piercing while the lift took me back up to Tristan's floor. Them giving me so much responsibility was a huge sign of trust, one I didn't think I was ever going to get, let alone so quickly. It felt good to finally have a purpose and know that I was actually going to be doing something that mattered.

I was desperately trying to not let all of my walls down and let them in. Having fun was one thing, but actually letting them in was a completely separate thing. And it was terrifying to think about. These guys were strangers a couple of weeks ago, and now here I was, sleeping with one of them, fooling around with another, and trying my hardest to get the third to cave as well.

And no matter how much I told myself I wasn't starting to feel anything for them, it was a lie. I could feel myself getting comfortable. I looked forward to the back-and-forth with Elliot, the sweet touches from Tristan, and Seb's crazy possessiveness. I saw a bit of myself in all of them, and it made me feel like I could finally be myself. Like I finally had a place where I could belong.

Like calls to like.

The doors opened, and I made my way to Tristan's office. I probably should've knocked, but that wasn't really my style. Tristan looked up as I entered and held a tattooed finger to his lips. A voice was coming through the speaker on his phone. He was laid back, the top few buttons of his shirt undone, sleeves rolled up on his strong forearms, and his hair uncharacteristically disheveled. He looked hot as hell, and my pussy seemed to take notice.

He pressed a button that I assumed muted the call and said, "Last meeting. I'll be done in a moment and we can head out to meet the others at the loft. Make yourself comfortable, love." He clicked the button again and answered the guy on the phone.

I smirked at him before locking the door and then slowly popping the button on my jeans and pulling down the zipper. His eyes darkened and watched the movement. I kicked off my boots and turned around before I slid my jeans down my legs, bending over and giving him a show. I turned around and watched him lick his lips. I lifted my shirt over my head and let it fall to the floor. The lace bralette and matching panties I had worn were a deep red and flattered my curves.

His eyes never left my body as I slowly walked over to him. He was still vaguely answering the guy's questions on the phone, but I knew he was barely paying attention to anything that wasn't me in that moment.

"What are you doing?" he mouthed.

I just smiled and knelt in between his legs. He was already hard, his cock pressing firmly against his pants. I unbuckled his belt and he lifted his hips so that I could pull his pants and boxers down. His cock sprang free, the vein pulsing and waiting for me. I looked up at him from under my eyelashes and brought my finger to my mouth to tell him to be quiet before taking him completely in my mouth. He twitched beneath me and groaned.

"Do you not like that?" the guy's voice came across the speaker. I smiled around his dick and dragged my teeth up his shaft. He hissed through his teeth but managed to pull himself together enough to answer.

"Yes, Charles, that's completely fine. Look, I've got to go," he said, and I let his head come out of my mouth with an audible *pop*. He jerked again. "Something's come up. I'll touch base with you tomorrow." Before poor Charles could even get a word in, Tristan had hung up the phone.

"What're you doing, you little minx?" His voice was

rough, and it went straight to my girl downstairs. I stood and ran my hands through his blond hair as I climbed on top of him, sliding my legs through the holes of the armrests.

"You looked so hot just sitting here in your big office, holding all the power. It did things to me," I moaned, grabbing his hand. Pushing my panties to the side, I ran his fingers through my soaked slit. He moaned like it was the sexiest thing he had ever felt which got me even wetter. "I thought maybe I could thank you for everything you've given me today."

I kissed him and stroked his cock through my folds, wetting him with my own excitement. His hands gripped my waist, and his tongue explored my mouth. He tasted like whiskey and power, and I soaked it up. I slowly, inch by inch, let him slip inside of me. He filled me up, stretching my walls in the most delicious way. I was panting by the time he was in me to the hilt. I started moving my hips, grinding down onto him like he was my only lifeline.

"You feel so good, baby girl," he murmured against my mouth. "This tight little cunt was made for me." One of his arms slipped around my waist and pulled me closer, causing my clit to rub against him, and I whimpered into his lips. His other hand freed a nipple and began to gently twirl and pinch, sending electricity down my spine. "Play with yourself," he commanded. I was so wet that when my fingers found my clit they slipped and circled around it easily. A heat was building deep inside of me, and I couldn't stop it.

"Tristan," I whispered, my head leaning against his, our breaths mixing and mingling.

"Do you need to come, love?" I nodded, and I heard a pitiful moan slip through my lips. Jesus, these men turned me into mush.

"Please," I begged.

"Go on, then. Let me see you come apart on my cock." He tweaked my other nipple painfully, and I fell apart. Heat sliced through my entire body, setting every muscle on fire in the most exquisite way. I screamed through it, throwing my head back and letting it wash over my body. Tristan sucked a nipple into his mouth and drew circles around it with his tongue, seeing me through each delicious moment of my orgasm.

He took the other one in his mouth as I came back down to earth. He bit it, hard, and I yelped and slapped him. His eyes darkened, and a terrifying smile slid across his mouth. His hands slid from my waist, up over my ribs, my breasts, and settled around my throat, holding me in place on top of him. He leaned forward and licked up the side of my face. Why that was such a turn-on, I had no idea.

"That's the only time you will ever get away with that, understood?" He squeezed my throat for emphasis. I smiled just as dangerously as he was.

"Or what?" I asked, breathless. He stood, bringing us both out of the chair before pulling me off him and bending me over his desk, his hand on the back of my neck. My face was painfully pressed onto a stack of papers, but my pussy had never been wetter. The anticipation was killing me. I heard the jingle of his belt and the sliding of fabric. I clenched and moaned, knowing what was coming.

"Stay. Still." I gripped the edge of the desk until I felt my knuckles go white. "Count."

And then I heard it before I felt it. The sharp slap of his belt across my ass echoed through the room and had my cunt throbbing with need.

"One," I whispered.

"Louder."

"One!"

Another smack. "Two!" Another. "Three!" Another. "Four!" Another. "Five!"

I felt tears slide down my cheeks and onto the papers beneath my face. My ass was on fire, but I was absolutely soaked. It was dripping down my thighs, and it took everything in me to not move to rub them together to try and quell the need for a release. I heard him toss his belt to the side. He ran his hands over the marks he had left, and I jumped from the sting.

"What a good girl you were, poppet." I mewled, hoping his hands were going to trail lower where I needed him. "Your ass looks so pretty with my marks all over it." He sank to his knees behind me and licked me from clit to ass. I pushed back onto his face, needing more. He licked me again and again, swirling the tip of his tongue around my puckered hole before dipping it inside. I moaned so loudly I felt it vibrate through the desk.

He stuck a finger inside my pussy, coating it in my cream while his tongue continued its invasion on my ass. I was pushing back on him, grinding on his face as much as I could without coming off the desk. I was desperate for it, moaning and whimpering, absolutely coming apart for him.

His tongue left but was quickly replaced with his finger, still soaked from my folds. He pushed it in slowly, giving me time to adjust. It went in knuckle by knuckle. He worked me into a fit of lust, and when he added another finger, I was breathless, gasping for air, begging for more.

"Tristan," I pleaded. He stood and slowly withdrew his fingers. Without warning, he slammed his dick into my pussy. I cried out, my nails digging hard into the wood of the desk. He crashed into me with so much force I thought I felt the desk move across the carpet. He pulled out of me, and I felt the head of his cock press against my ass.

"Deep breaths, baby girl. Relax for me." I relaxed, pushing back onto him, needing him to fill me in any way he could. I was so close to coming just from his belt alone that I was fucking desperate for him. His head slid all the way in, and he groaned. He was going too slow. I needed him inside of me.

"Just fuck me, already," I said, trying and successfully pushing back on him a few more inches. He laughed darkly and reached around my hips to tease my clit, sending me into an all-out frenzy. Then with one punishing thrust, he was fully sheathed inside of my ass. I cried out in a sweet mixture of pain and pleasure. He gave me all of two seconds to adjust before he pulled out and pushed back in, all the while rubbing my clit in teasing circles.

"I'm...I'm gonna..." I couldn't even form coherent sentences. I was so lost in what he was doing to my body, the heat spreading through every inch of my skin, that I was speechless. His dick literally made me dumb. With each thrust, I was lost further to the orgasm building deep in my belly. The sound of his heavy breaths, his moaning every time I squeezed him, sent me into a spiral.

"Do it," he said in between breaths. "Come for me." He smacked my already sore ass cheeks with one hand and squeezed my clit with the other. Stars exploded across my vision, and I swore I blacked out for a moment, coming out of my body before settling back in. Every single nerve in my body pulsed with it.

Tristan's thrusts became faster and more erratic. He pulled out, and a moment later, I felt his cum shoot across my ass, hot on my already stinging skin.

"Jesus Christ, Scarlet," he said as he rubbed his release into my skin. "What a fucking sight you are." I finally relaxed against the desk, completely spent. That was some of the best sex I had ever had in my life. I heard him pull his pants back on, but I was too exhausted to move and a little nervous to try sitting down.

"Stay here, sweetheart," he said before landing a kiss on my cheek. "I'm just going to go get something to clean you up with, okay?"

I nodded and sighed, completely content. I was so well and truly fucked, and not just in the most literal meaning of the word. With each day, I kept finding myself more and more tangled up in their world and with them. I couldn't stop myself. Everything about them called out to me. I wanted to be with them all the time. Their darkness made my shadows seem not as dark.

"Alright, love," Tristan said, coming back into the office with a wet cloth and a few other items. "Let's get you cleaned up and go get you some food, yeah?" I smiled and nodded from where I was on the desk. He bent down to my level and kissed me hard, pouring into it all the feelings we were both too afraid to say out loud. He kissed my nose and then, with gentle hands, cleaned me up before helping me get dressed.

CHAPTER
twenty four

TRISTAN

Scarlet had winced when she climbed onto the bike for our trip to the loft, and I wondered for a moment if I had been too rough with her. But thinking back to how she had been whimpering underneath me, panting, her body begging for it, I pushed that thought to the back of my mind. The way her skin had reddened and puckered under the force of my belt had snapped something in my brain. In that moment, I had lived and breathed for her, for the way her body responded to me.

There was no going back now. This wild little creature was mine, ours, and I wasn't going to let her go. The way she kissed me back afterwards had confessed far more than I think she thought it did. She may not have been ready to say it out loud yet, but she wanted to be with us. She wanted this life for herself. And I wanted it for her. I needed her to want it.

The loft we kept in the city was only a few blocks away from the Tower, and when the lift doors opened up to our penthouse, the smell of Rico's Italian came flooding into the lift. I was starving after all the work I had just put into her. Scarlet's eyes roamed across the wide expanse of the penthouse, drinking it all in. I would never get sick of looking at her.

"You guys really like to flaunt that you have money, don't you?" She smirked and walked inside, making herself at home. "Ever heard of investing?"

"Trust me, love, this is a small drop in the ocean that is our wealth. You don't have to worry about us."

She looked at me over her shoulder with a smile and then sauntered off, swaying her ass with each step. I watched her walking away, letting my mind drift back to how it had looked with my dick inside of it less than thirty minutes ago. My cock sprang back to life and twitched in my pants. I adjusted myself and followed her the rest of the way in.

"Hey there, hot stuff," I heard Sebastian call from the kitchen. A loud smack was followed by Scarlet's scream, and I laughed to myself at how much that must've hurt her still-raw skin. I walked into the kitchen just in time to watch her rear back and slap Seb right across the face, a handprint forming almost instantly.

"After what your pal over there did to my ass earlier, you don't get to touch it for days. Understood?" Her finger wasn't even an inch away from his nose, but his grin grew into a sick smile. I rolled my eyes. Never present a challenge to Seb because he was always going to push the boundaries. And he normally won.

"Bad idea, princess," Elliot said from the table. "Seb loves a good challenge. Especially when it involves pain."

"I'm serious, Sebastian."

"Ooh, she said my full name! You must've done a number on her, T!" He picked her up around the waist and gave her a tight hug before putting her back on the ground and taking his seat at the table.

"We will not be talking about any of that nonsense at the dinner table!" Melody walked out of the back of the loft. "Mind your manners," she said and swatted Seb on the back of the head as she passed. Scarlet's cheeks burned red. I kissed her on her head before sitting down and pulling her down roughly onto my lap. She flinched but slowly relaxed back into my chest.

"You're hogging her!" Sebastian whined from the other side of the table.

"You had her all last night and this morning," I countered. "I get her for the afternoon."

"Will you two stop bickering over her like children?" Elliot asked in his grumpiest voice. He wasn't fooling me though. I had seen the way he had looked at her in that warehouse while she was kicking ass. And ever since that night, he had been asking about her nonstop and stealing glances at her whenever she wasn't looking. He was interested, he just didn't know how to voice it…yet.

"How about we stop talking about Scarlet like she isn't here and eat?" Melody asked at the head of the table. She started opening up all of the catering containers that we had had delivered from Rico's, intensifying the smell of garlic and cheese.

I grabbed a plate for Scarlet, filled her plate up as full as it would go, and sat it down in front of her.

"Eat," I said. She rolled her eyes at me and grabbed her plate before standing up and taking the seat next to me. She winced as her ass came into contact with the hard wood of the chair, which was exactly why I had been holding her. My legs would have been much easier to sit on than that chair, but the girl was stubborn as a mule.

"Melody, how long have you worked for these guys?"

"Going on about six years now, right?" I nodded. "I've been through a lot with these guys. They've really been so sweet to me. Gave me this job, got me a nice apartment, and they always make sure they pay me a visit every now and then. Well," she said with a pointed look at each of us, "until recently, that is."

Scarlet laughed. "Sorry, I think you can blame that one on me. I hear I'm a bit of a handful. And they've had to play the role of babysitter a lot lately."

"You remember that time Mel shot Elliot?" Sebastian blurted, suddenly laughing his ass off. "Mel, you have got to tell that story."

I rolled my eyes. That story had been told so many times I was genuinely shocked that Seb could still find it funny. Scarlet's eyes widened and swiveled to Elliot. I could tell she was trying really hard to not just burst out laughing in his face. Probably smart of her not to, honestly. That story was a real sore spot for him.

"And how did that happen?" God, she was cute when she was trying not to laugh. Elliot grumbled and shoved more food in his mouth, refusing to look up from his plate.

If I didn't know any better, I thought, *I would think he's embarrassed she's finding this out.*

"I had told Mel that we were out on a job, and she was keeping watch over some stuff for me back at the Tower," I started.

"And I was told that no matter what, they wouldn't be going back there." Mel gave Elliot a hard look, and he sat back in his chair, arms crossed.

"And I didn't think you would mistake me for a common thug and shoot me."

"At least it wasn't a fatal shot," Sebastian laughed.

"It could've been! Crazy woman shot me inches away from my damn heart!"

Melody laughed, and I saw Scarlet bite back a laugh.

"Poor thing," Scar said and winked at Elliot. The bastard cracked a smile at her, and I almost choked. She was definitely getting under his skin and had been ever since he'd seen her get shot for us in that warehouse. It didn't surprise me that that's what it took for him to see her as anything other than a burden.

Elliot had a lot of faults, but he was loyal to those who were loyal to him. And when he had seen her burst through those doors after killing multiple men for us and then continue to fight for us, risking her own life…I thought maybe something had clicked into place. Whether he liked it or not, she had saved our asses, and he had to respect that.

"You know," Scarlet said as she shoveled another bite of food in her mouth. That woman could eat. I had no idea where she put all of it. She had put on a little muscle over the past few weeks training with Elliot, but she was still so small. Suddenly, the image of throwing her around in the bedroom popped into my mind, and I almost choked on my food. She patted my back with a grin that made me think she knew where my head was but continued. "I have had a lot of Italian food growing up because my *bunica* is Italian, but this shit is amazing."

"It's Rico's." She turned her pretty eyes onto me. "It's our favorite place. We've been in business with him for a long time now."

"In business with," she said while making air quotes with her fingers.

"I think it's the nicest way of putting things, yes. Business."

She smiled and then looked around the room, taking in the view from the floor-to-ceiling windows in the living room. "Is this where you guys normally live? When you aren't having to babysit me out in the country?"

"Normally, yes."

"It's kind of cold. I think I prefer the manor."

"Normally we take turns going out there," Sebastian said. "If one of us needs a break or wants a vacation for a few days, we go out there and chill. Elliot and

I can't stand the incessant pounding Tristan does on his drums when he's pissy, so Tristan tends to go there more often than we do."

"You boys are more temperamental than teenage girls," Melody mumbled as she took a long sip of wine.

"I've noticed that," Scarlet said through a smile.

"They better be minding their manners."

Scarlet snorted at that and then stood. She looked around at all three of us. I saw Melody smile behind her drink as she watched Scarlet hold all the power over us. All three of us watched and waited, like her little lapdogs. Even Elliot, who was trying not to be as obvious about it, was a little more on edge waiting to see who she was about to call on.

"Elliot," she said, locking her eyes onto him. I watched his gaze slide onto her out of the corner of my eye. Jealousy tried to take root in my gut, but I pushed it down. If I was going to make her stay, we needed to make this work. She wanted all of us, and I was happy to see my friends happy. So I needed to get over my mental hang-ups and let this run its course. "Take me for a tour?"

Elliot sat there for a moment, staring at her. I could've cut the tension with a knife. We were all watching him, waiting to see what he would say. I honestly figured he would give her a snarky comment or tell her to go fuck herself.

"Alright," he said and stood up, throwing his hair into a bun. "I'll take a turn being your little bitch boy." He walked around the table, and as he passed her, she grabbed his arm and sprang up onto his back like a fucking monkey. He tilted to the side and swore before helping her hop the rest of the way up onto his back.

We all watched them go, Elliot telling her this and that about the loft before disappearing down the hallway. I stared after them for a minute, and when I turned around, both Melody and Sebastian were looking at me.

"What?"

"We are well and truly fucked," Sebastian said.

"Yes, you are," Melody agreed. "What do you intend to do with her? Her family isn't going to just give up trying to take hold of this city—*your* city."

"I know," I said, running my hand over the scruff that had started to form. "Whatever we do…"

"We can't lose her," Sebastian finished for me.

"We can't lose her," I agreed.

"Then don't," Mel said.

CHAPTER
twenty five

SCARLET

After we got home, Seb dropped onto his knees on the wood floors and begged to be able to sleep with me for the night. Elliot rolled his eyes but ruffled my hair, and he walked past us and down the hall, off to do god knew what with the rest of his night.

"I wanted to go play in the music room anyway. I have some shit to sort out." Tristan kissed my cheek and then left Seb and me alone. I looked down at him, his brown eyes full of mischief.

"Seb, no sex." He pouted. "I'm serious. My ass is on fire, and *she* is sore."

"Fine," he whined and picked me up as he stood. "Let's get your ass taken care of first and then nothing but cuddles. Pinky promise." I wrapped my pinky around his and then leaned my head against his shoulder. I could've walked to my bedroom, but when he was offering to carry me, why would I put out the effort? It was nice to be taken care of sometimes.

We lay in bed with my back to his front while he twirled his fingers through my hair. He had rubbed ointment gently across my stinging flesh before we both crawled into bed. I was physically, mentally, and sexually exhausted from the day, and feeling his solid body against mine had me drifting off within minutes.

"Scarlet." His low voice jolted me out of sleep, and I felt him laugh behind me.

"Yes?" I looked over my shoulder, and he nuzzled into my hair.

"I want you to *want* to stay."

I took a deep breath. I wasn't sure what to say. I figured that topic was going to come up eventually, seeing as I was getting closer and closer with all of them. And they seemed to be letting me in more each day. But would I actually want to stay with them if I didn't have to? I didn't know the answer to that.

"I want a life," I finally managed.

"You could have a life with us if you promised not to run away, little pet." He pulled me tighter to him and kissed my hair.

"Because the smartest dogs always come back?" I was half-joking, but he didn't find it funny. He sighed and grabbed my chin, forcing me to look at him through the darkness.

"Because we need you. And I think you need us."

He kissed my nose. "Now stop making me angry or I'll put your mouth to good use."

I rolled back over and pulled the blanket under my chin. I waited until his breathing was slow and even before letting myself drift back off. But I needed to make a decision…and soon. Was I going to just give in and try to be happy in their world? Or was I going to try and run?

I wanted to have a life outside of them if I stayed. They couldn't expect me to go from building to building, always one of them by my side, without having any freedom whatsoever.

God, I missed having Kenna to talk to. She had to be seriously freaking out over all of this. She knew enough to keep her mouth shut and not go looking for me, but I knew she would be terrified. And I had been so caught up in my own shit I hadn't even tried to convince the guys to let me send her a message. I needed to let her know that I was okay.

I took a few deep breaths and tried to tell myself I didn't have to decide what to do immediately. I was still injured, still technically on the run from my family, and it's not like I had it so rough with the guys. I lay there and listened to Seb's slow breathing, letting it calm me. I was beginning to depend on them much more than I had intended to.

Seb's clean scent calmed me down, and I settled into him. I had never been one to cuddle, but something about these idiots made my insides turn to mush. It wasn't something I would ever admit to them. They didn't need to know that they had any kind of emotional sway over me. I brought his hand to my mouth and kissed his knuckles before finally drifting off to sleep.

CHAPTER
twenty six

SEBASTIAN

"Hey," I heard someone whisper. I instantly swung out my free arm, but it was caught mid-strike. "It's Tristan, you nance."

I rolled my eyes. He had the weirdest fucking sayings.

"You mean 'nonce,'" I whispered back.

"Whatever. Come on, something's happened."

I groaned but slowly and quietly pulled myself free from Scarlet. She had turned around and curled herself into my chest, gripping tightly onto my worn T-shirt. Once I worked her fingers free, I was able to roll out of her bed and pad silently across the floor. If I was gone too long, she would wake up. She would never admit it, but she needed one of us to sleep with her. I'd learned early on that her nightmares visited her often, and it seemed like they got better the longer she was with us.

I knew she thought we were all just heartless gangsters, but she was starting to worm her way into our hearts. I wasn't lying when I told her I wanted her to want to stay with us. If we could trust her, we would happily let her have her freedom back. But she'd need protection out there once word got out that she was with the Triad. She couldn't go back to living the life she had before, not that I thought she would want to. Who wants to be constantly on the run, living in slums, and watching your back?

"We've been hit. The loft in the city was broken into and trashed beyond belief," Tristan said as I joined both him and Elliot in the hallway. I clicked Scarlet's door shut.

"What the fuck? Her family?" I asked, nodding my head towards her room.

"Has to be," Elliot said in hushed tones. "We don't have a bounty on our heads with anyone else. And Derek wouldn't have the balls."

"Anyway, we need to go down there and take a look."

"Who is staying back with Scar?" I asked.

"There are five of our guys here, Seb," Tristan said, rubbing his eyes. He could act like he was pissed I was asking, but I knew he was worried about leaving her here alone just as much as I was.

"Five isn't enough," I countered.

"Five is fucking plenty, Seb," Elliot groaned.

"All three of us need to go. If anyone sees us out

there this late at night, separated, they're going to be suspicious or see it as a perfect opportunity to strike." Tristan gave both of us a stern look. "We go together, yes?"

Elliot nodded, but I looked back at her door one more time, debating on how much I actually wanted to fight them.

"We could just bring her," I said half-heartedly. I knew they wouldn't go for it, and I really didn't think it was the best idea either. She needed her rest, and I didn't like the idea of keeping her up all night just to go take a look around a vandalized loft.

"Really? You really want to wake her up in the middle of the night? She would probably chop your balls off. You know how she loves her sleep," Elliot said. I cringed, and I swore my balls shrunk up inside of me. She definitely would, my lethal little thing.

"Fine. But I want someone outside her door for when she wakes up wondering why we left."

"Done. Get dressed. We leave in five."

CHAPTER
twenty seven

TRISTAN

I told the guys staying behind to make sure every door was locked, bolted, and watched closely. Matthew, the one I trusted the most out of the five, was stuck on door duty should Scarlet wake up and wonder where the hell we had gone. I couldn't believe the effort we were going through just to make sure she didn't get upset. We told the guys that we wanted her watched to make sure she didn't try to run, but between the three of us, we knew they were keeping her comfortable and safe.

We were worried about her.

I didn't know how it had gotten to this point. From the moment I'd seen her big blue eyes, I knew she was going to be trouble. She was broken, and we were going to try and heal her. I just hoped she was able to heal us as well.

CHAPTER
twenty eight

SCARLET

I rolled over to an empty bed and sat straight up. Seb never left me alone when he was staying in my bed. The sappy idiot could deny it all he wanted, but I knew he worried about my nightmares. I felt around the bed, but it was cold. He'd been gone for a while.

My stomach was instantly in knots. Something wasn't right. My feet softly hit the floor, and I made my way across the hardwood to put on some pants before wandering out into the house. Surely they hadn't just left me. They never left me without at least one of them babysitting.

I turned the doorknob as slowly as I possibly could. I was terrified to make a noise. I hadn't been this scared since I first ran away. Back then I was listening to every little noise I heard, assuming that someone had finally found me. This felt far too similar to that. The ghosts of scars that would never quite leave me alone. I felt my heart racing in my chest, and the blood roaring in my head with panicked frenzy was drowning out anything else useful I might be able to hear.

When I finally got the balls to open the door, the hallway was empty. They hadn't even left anyone to sit by the door. What the fuck had happened? A flashback of that night, that guy on top of me, flew through my mind, and I pushed it back to where it came from.

I may have only known them a few weeks, but they wouldn't leave me. They weren't my family. There was no way they had hired someone to take care of me, to take me back to that place. The panic crept its way up my spine, begging me to stay hidden in my room. But the overly confident side of my brain won, telling me to go find one of them. Because they had to be in the house.

They wouldn't leave me.

Making my way down the long hallway, I peeked into each of their rooms, hoping to find at least one of them asleep.

Nothing.

The house was eerily quiet. I went slowly down the stairs, trying to look around through the dark and find one of their guys. There were always men hanging around, watching the house, and watching me. But I still hadn't seen a single person. At the bottom of the stairs, I stepped in something wet, and any sense of calm I may have had was completely erased. I felt the tears threaten and my throat constrict.

Fuck, fuck, fuck.

I took a couple of steps and flipped on the light. When I looked down at my foot, it was stained red with blood. My stomach flipped, and I turned around slowly to survey the room.

One, two, three, four, and five men. All lying on the floor. All dead. Gunshot in between each of their eyes. Whoever had done this had been expertly trained. And they had ruined Tristan's new carpet. He was going to be pissed.

"Where the fuck are the boys?" I whispered to myself.

I needed to find weapons. I wasn't that weak little girl anymore that was so easy to overtake a few years ago. I was smarter, stronger. And I could take care of myself. Fuck those assholes that wore me down, made me feel safe and welcome. Fuck them for breaking down my walls and making me believe that I could actually belong somewhere.

I turned the light back off and crept around the foyer, rubbing my foot on the rug near the door to try and get as much of the blood off it that I could. I didn't need anyone tracking me through the house. I knew the guys kept weapons stashed throughout the home just in case. Keeping my breaths as slow and even as I could, I made my way through the hallways towards Tristan's music room.

Before I could make it there, I heard a thump come from behind me, and as I whipped around to see what it was, a fist connected with my face, smacking my head against the wall. Stars flew through my vision, but I swung out and kicked in the direction it came from. My foot connected, and I pushed as hard as I could. I heard him grunt and fall to the floor.

"Bitch," he swore.

"That's me," I shot back and took off running towards the front of the house. I needed to get to the garage and get the fuck out of here. I didn't know if this was them or if it was my family. Hell, it could've been the gang whose drug operation we took down together. But it didn't matter. Whoever it was, I needed to run.

I grabbed onto the top of the bannister to swing my body around and head towards the kitchen where the garage door was. The moment my body made the turn, a hand gripped a fist full of my hair and yanked back. I cried out and went down onto the carpet with a thud, the air whooshing out of my lungs.

"Motherfucker," I wheezed, trying to roll away and get back on my feet. I needed to get back up to be able to have a chance at fighting the asshole.

"That's me," he taunted and then kicked me in the ribs. I swore I felt one crack in half. I screamed. He kicked me in my bad shoulder, and another scream flew out of my throat. "Aren't you going to fight back? Poor little slut. Not so much of a threat without your boys and your guns, are you?"

I gripped my side and rolled over, trying to pick myself up. I managed to get onto my knees before his fist flew and smacked me right across my face. Blood filled my mouth, and I spat it out onto the carpet.

"Stupid bitch," he yelled as he kicked me in the

stomach again. I heaved and fell back onto the floor. He crouched over me, pinning my arms to my sides and straddling my hips. Panic flared in my chest. This was not going to happen again. I thrashed under him, ignoring the sharp pain in my ribs.

"Get off of me!" I shouted, working my arms free from his grip.

"Need some help?" A shadow of another person walked into the room, and I thrashed harder. I knew what could easily happen when it was two against one. I was not going down without a fight. I finally worked an arm free and swung up at the guy on top of me, my fist connecting with his jaw while he was distracted.

"Cunt!"

"Enough," the other guy said before I saw the shadow of his boot swing out. I braced for the kick and felt white-hot pain as it connected with my head, and everything faded to black.

CHAPTER
twenty nine

TRISTAN

"I thought you said more of our guys would be here," Elliot murmured into the dark. It was cold outside, fully winter, and the wind was biting through my layers. I looked up at the building. It was completely dark. It didn't seem out of the ordinary for the building to be dark in the middle of the night, but the fact that the loft wasn't lit up was troubling. Our people were supposed to be waiting on us.

"I did. They were supposed to be here. Maybe the power is out up there."

"Or maybe this is a trap and we're fucked," Seb said.

"I'd prefer to think the power is out."

"Let's just go," Elliot finally said, pushing his way past us and into the building. It was dark as hell inside with all of the staff gone for the night. I had told Melody on the phone to send everyone home, including herself. She was leaving to go back to her own apartment when I got off the phone with her to wake Seb up. I didn't need anyone getting caught in any potential crossfire just because they had to work the late shift.

We pressed the button for the lift, and as the door opened, I sighed. Blood. We all swore at the same time. We all knew that this wasn't just a break-in anymore. It was an attack.

"How many of our people are we going to find dead up there?" Seb asked.

"If they got all of them? At least ten." I walked into the lift first, and they followed. The ride up to the top floor was long, with the metallic stench of blood filling the air.

"Alright," Elliot said as the lights indicated we were almost there. "Eyes open. Guns up. No one dies."

"No one dies," Seb and I both repeated.

The doors shifted open into the loft, and it was dark, really dark. There was one light still hanging from the ceiling, flickering and buzzing like a fucking horror film. We all gripped our guns, instantly on alert. The adrenaline rushed through my veins and made me hope there would be someone there waiting for us. I was ready. After seeing Elliot stabbed and Scarlet shot, I was out for revenge. I wanted to taste their blood on my tongue and watch the life drain from their pitiful fucking eyes.

No one hurt my people and lived to tell the tale.

We ushered ourselves out into the open space,

keeping our heads on a swivel, making sure no one was lurking in the shadows. Tables were overturned, the carpets squished with blood, and the walls were peppered with bullet holes. They didn't go easy on us. They were here to make a point. I did a quick head count of the bodies on the floor. Seven. Some I could tell were ours, and others I had never seen before.

"I'll check the rest of the open space. You and Seb go check the back bedrooms. We'll go upstairs together," Elliot ordered.

I nodded and headed off towards the bedrooms, Seb in tow. After checking through each one and getting the all clear from Elliot, we all headed upstairs together, Elliot leading all three of us.

Three more of our guys were dead at the top of the landing. As we made our way down the hall, we had to step over four more. Two were ours, two were unknown.

The last door to check was our gym, and the wooden door was littered with bullet holes. Elliot looked back at us, knowing that this was the last place anyone could be if they were still in the loft and alive. He turned the knob quietly and then thrust it open, quickly taking stock of the room before he stopped dead in his tracks.

Even in the dim light, I could see him turn white as a sheet. I saw him swallow.

"El," I started, but he turned towards me and held up his hand.

"What the fuck is going on?" Seb asked, pushing past me. As he got to the doorway though, Elliot grabbed him. But it was too late. Seb screamed. It was a sound so excruciating that my teeth ground together and my body went cold. I felt nothing but dread as I watched Seb's face contort in pain as he choked on a sob.

"No," he whispered and pushed his way out of Elliot's arms and into the room.

CHAPTER
thirty

ELLIOT

"Seb, we have got to go," Tristan said again as Seb held Melody's lifeless form in his arms. Melody. Sweet, loving Melody. Put up with our shit Melody. I found her propped against the wall, gun still in her limp hand, her body riddled with bullet holes. The moment I saw her, my entire body had gone cold.

"I will break every single bone in their body. After that, I will skin them like fucking animals." Sebastian had been rambling and making promises I knew he would keep. "You said you told her to get out!" He was yelling at Tristan.

"I did, Seb. Last I spoke to her, she was going down to tell everyone else to leave. She told me she would leave right after. She must've come back up for something and got caught in the crossfire."

"This has to be a diversion," I said, thinking out loud. "They'd have to know that we would all show up. So why aren't they here?"

"I don't know," Tristan said from his crouching position next to Seb, who was still running his hands through her matted hair, whispering into her ear. We needed to get him to focus on something else or he was going to break. Seb was the most emotional of all of us. He got attached the easiest, loved the hardest. Melody's death was going to consume him if we didn't get him out of that room.

"What if they wanted to get us out of the manor?" I asked. Worry washed through my stomach. We had left Scarlet there.

"Scarlet?" Tristan asked. "You think they're going for Scarlet."

"I do."

Sebastian's head tilted up and towards us. The look on his face would have made a lesser person shit themselves. He took a few steadying breaths and laid Melody on the floor and closed her eyes. I swallowed at the lump in my throat.

"If they lay a fucking finger on our girl, I will burn their entire city to ashes." Seb stood and wiped at his face, smearing Mel's blood across his cheeks in the process.

"We need to get back there in case that's where they're headed." I turned on my heel and made my way through the broken loft, leaving behind my grief for the time being. I could feel both of them behind me, their anger radiating off them in waves.

I didn't love the girl. Hell, I didn't like her on the best of days, but she had proven herself useful and loyal over the past few weeks. I was getting used to having her around. Hearing her laughter and her sailor mouth booming through the house on a regular basis. Her naked, tattooed legs swinging from the counter in the mornings while she drank her coffee. The way her dark hair made her blue eyes look like ice sometimes.

I shook my head. Sebastian was right. If they laid a finger on *our* girl, we wouldn't stop until their entire city was underground. Whether I wanted to admit it or not, Scarlet had gotten under my skin. I had fought it for as long as I could, but somehow that infuriating woman had wormed her way into my life.

Tristan was calling the cleanup crew behind me, giving special instructions for Melody. Each man was to be returned to his family, if he had one. If he didn't, we would take care of it and give him a proper funeral. But Melody? Melody was our family. She was to be held until this mess was over and we could give her a send-off worthy of who she was to us.

We all squeezed back into the lift, and Sebastian hung his head. He was biting back all the tears he wanted to shed for Melody. He knew we needed to have clear heads going back to the manor. If this was all a ploy to get us out of the house, Scarlet could have already been gone. If he lost two women in one night, I pitied the people he took it out on. That bastard put both of us to shame when it came to torture. And the way he looked at Scarlet, the way he cared for her… they were in for some real fucking pain.

"They can't have even known where we were keeping her," Tristan said almost to himself.

"I don't know how they would've found out," I agreed. "We used our most trusted people out there."

"Emily?" Sebastian asked with death in his voice.

"No," Tristan said. "I paid her far too much money for her silence and shipped her off. I saw the way Scarlet looked at her. Emily wouldn't have lasted five more minutes around all of us." Tristan grinned, and I laid my head back on the wall of the lift. "I think she likes us."

"You think?" I asked through a laugh. "She likes you two, that's for sure."

"Shut up, El. You don't see the way she looks at you when you aren't paying attention. She wants your attention just as much as she wants ours." Sebastian grinned and crossed his arms. "And you're starting to give in."

I grunted and let the conversation drop. The ride back to the manor was going to be a long one. If we got there and Scarlet was gone, or worse, dead, we were going to have a long road ahead of us.

CHAPTER
thirty one

SEBASTIAN

"*Scarlet!*" My voice was hoarse with the effort of shouting her name over and over again as I made my way through the house. There was nothing but death. I checked every single room, closet, and cupboard I could find. She wasn't in the house.

"Sebastian, she isn't here," Tristan called from downstairs. But I was too busy searching her room for the fifth time that I couldn't focus on whatever the fuck they were doing down there. "We need to figure out who did this!" He called up again. "Let's sit down and make some phone calls!"

I sighed and took one last glance around her room before running downstairs. Tristan was already on the phone with whoever the fuck he thought was going to have some sort of answer. I was fuming. I couldn't sit down. Elliot was sitting in one of the armchairs in the living room, staring off into space and chewing on his lips, the only amount of emotion would let anyone see.

Tristan was in a heated discussion with someone in Spanish, so I could only assume he had reached someone in Derek's crew. His face turned red, and the vein on his neck popped. He threw his phone against the fireplace and watched the screen spiderweb.

Great. Good thing we have all of our contacts backed up elsewhere.

The house phone rang.

We all looked at each other and then in the general direction of the phone. We only had one landline phone in the entire home, and it was for the staff to use. None of us had ever even touched the thing. On the third ring, I was out of the living room and into the hallway where it hung on the wall. Tristan and Elliot ran in behind me.

"What?" I asked into the receiver.

"What would it mean to you if I said we had your little Romani pet?"

I held the phone out for the other guys to hear. "Why would I believe you?"

The voice on the other end sighed. "Was the five guards murdered and your missing bitch not enough? Fine." I heard the crunching of gravel in the background and then what sounded like a door opening. *"No eres tan fuerte ahora, ah perra?"*

I looked at Tristan. I didn't understand a lick of Spanish.

"He just called her a bitch," Tristan mouthed. The

vein in Tristan's neck looked like it was about to burst. I was having a hard time not cracking the phone in half. And Elliot stood there, still as a statue, staring at the phone like he would jump through it.

There was a shuffle on the other side of the phone and then a grunt as something hit the gravel. That's when she screamed. All three of us tensed simultaneously at that bloodcurdling sound. I saw red, and every muscle in my body poised for a fight. I was going to torture them for hours and then light pieces of them on fire and watch their flesh bubble and burn. I would break every little *fucking* bone in their pathetic bodies until they screamed for death.

"*Solo espera lo que tenemos planeado para ti.*" And then I heard him spit on her. He fucking spit on *my fucking woman.*

"He said something about waiting to see what he had planned for her," Tristan whispered.

"Let's go!" someone else called from further away. As I was about to ask what they wanted, he came back on.

"The warehouse." He hung up, and I looked up at Elliot and Tristan.

"We're going."

"Of course we're going," Elliot said. "We need to load up."

"You guys get what we need," Tristan said. "I'll call in backup." I nodded and followed Elliot towards our weapons room. "And Seb?" I looked at him over my shoulder. "You have free rein in there."

I smiled.

CHAPTER
thirty two

SCARLET

I came to with my arms tied behind my back and a gag in my mouth. My eyes were almost swollen shut, and my ribs were screaming. I tried to take calm breaths through my nose because the harder I tried, the harder it was to get air into my lungs. My face was wet with either tears or blood, I couldn't tell.

My legs were tied together at my knees and my ankles. I still had pants on, and I thanked whatever gods there were that it didn't seem like they had raped me while I was out cold. We were moving, and by the feel of things, I was in the boot of a car. It was pitch-black with two faint red lights shining in.

I could barely control my movements being tied up the way I was. With each brake and acceleration, I was rolled back and forth like a sack of potatoes, doing fucking wonders for my healing shoulder injury. I groaned and tried to stretch my legs as straight as I could get them. They were seizing up, which had to mean we had been traveling for a while if I was stuck in that position long enough for my muscles to cramp.

I groaned into the gag as they stretched and loosened. Being short was working to my advantage. I was able to get almost completely straightened out. But every time I took a breath, my ribs ached and made tears fall down my cheeks. They had definitely broken my ribs.

The car turned onto a gravel road, left or right, I couldn't tell, and didn't miss a single pothole. I was starting to think they were aiming for them just to see how much they could actually jostle me around. The car slowed and came to a halt, pushing me towards the back of the boot. I grunted when I rolled over on my injured shoulder, biting into whatever rag they had shoved into my mouth.

The car door opened, and heavy footsteps crunched back towards me. It was all I could do to not let myself spiral into a panic attack. I wanted to cry, but my mind wouldn't let me. I was too stubborn for that shit. I was not going down like a little bitch. I still didn't know who had taken me, whether it was my family or the druggies.

I had pushed it completely out of my mind that it could've been the guys. I wouldn't let myself think like that. There was no way they would have set this up. Something had to have taken them out of the house last minute. Something important or they never would've left me alone. I wasn't delusional. I didn't think they were so head over heels for me that I was considered one of them. But they cared enough that they wouldn't do something like this. It wasn't them.

And so it only left two options, and neither one was too appealing. If it was my family, I would more than likely be dead before the sun as up. If it was the gang, I had no idea what would happen. Torture was the first thing that came to mind. If they knew the guys had any kind of feelings for me, they could use that to their advantage. I shivered.

I counted the footsteps as they approached. When they paused at the door, I held my breath. The latch clicked open, and I was bathed in amber streetlight. The guy standing in front of me was wearing a ski mask over his face, and the light behind him made it impossible to make out anything about him. One hand held something to his face. A phone?

"*No eres tan fuerte ahora, ah perra?*"

I didn't speak Spanish, but I knew what *perra* meant. I was getting really sick and fucking tired of people calling me a bitch. I stared at him, refusing to look weak even if I was bound and gagged at his mercy. He reached down and pulled me out of the boot by my hair, my scalp screaming at the assault. My body flailed and fell hard onto the gravel. I couldn't help it; I screamed again. He shoved the boot shut and looked down at me.

"*Solo espera lo que tenemos planeado para ti.*" He spat on my face, and my temper flared. He was going to pay for that one with his life.

"Let's go," another guy said from the side of the car.

"The warehouse," he said into the phone and then hung up and put it in his pocket. With that, I was picked up and thrown over dude's shoulder, crushing my already broken ribs. Pain flared through every inch of my body, and when the blackness threatened at my vision, I welcomed it.

Surely the guys would come for me soon.

I just had to stay alive.

The next book in the series is available to pre-order here: Liars

ACKNOWLEDGMENTS

First, to the readers. Thank you for taking a chance on a first time author. You can never know how much it means to me that you gave me a chance to tell you a story. Thank you.

To Amber, my guardian angel. You have no idea how much you helped me and continue to help me through this process. Without you, I would be floating in the endless ocean that is self-publishing. Thank you for answering all my questions, listening to my rants, and reading everything that I sent your way. Thank you for taking time out of your own schedule to help inspire me and give me courage to do this. You are such a massive piece to the puzzle that is this book.

To the infamous group chat, you know who you all are. Thank you for the (somewhat) late night discussions, the endless support, and kicking my ass into gear when I needed it. Thank you for all the laughs and the rage sessions. I love each and every one of you with every piece of my heart. We did it! Look at us. Who would've thought?

To Michelle, my soul half. I love you more than words can express. Ever since I met you in that tiny uni classroom in York (too many years ago now to count), I have been head over heels for you. Your friendship has gotten me through so much in my life. You have been the person I can come to no matter what. Thank you for always being there, for always talking me down off the cliff, and for always keeping my name in your phone as Big Booty. It's the confidence boost I will always need.

To Abi, my amazing cover designer at Pink Elephant Designs. Girl, you have no idea how much I appreciated your infinite patience with me as I navigated through my first ever cover design. Thank you for putting up with my multiple emails and requests. You hit it out of the park. I could not be happier with this cover and I cannot wait for the next one.

To Sandra, my editor at One Love Editing. The edit you did on this book was amazing. Thank you for fixing all of those comma splices and changing every single yea to yeah. You'd have no idea I went to college for English.

To every single author that has communicated with me and encouraged me over the last six months, thank you. I never thought I would be here. But with all of your examples, I was able to push myself out of my comfort zone and make this happen. Thank you all for the amazing community you have created.

To all of you aspiring authors out there that may have taken the time to read these acknowledgements all the way through - don't give up. You can do this. Push yourself. And if you have any questions or need any moral support, come to me. I am here to give you as much hype as I can possibly give.

ABOUT
the author

Dana Isaly is a writer of dark romance, fantasy romance, and has also been known to dabble in poetry (it was a phase in college, leave her alone).

She was born in the Midwest and has been all over but now resides (begrudgingly) in Alabama. She is a lover of books, coffee, and rainy days. Dana is probably the only person in the writing community that is actually a morning person.

She swears too much, is way too comfortable on her TikTok, and believes that love is love is love.

You can find her on Instagram (@danaisalyauthorpage) or on Facebook with the same name. Honestly though, the best place to get in touch with her is on TikTok (@authordanaisaly) because she isn't great with any other social media.

ALSO BY
Dana Isaly

Liars (The Triad Series Book 2)

Flame and Starlight: releasing July 21, 2021

Games We Play

(Will also be available in audiobook with narration by vo.Eros)

Printed in Great Britain
by Amazon